*And we know that all things work
together for good to them that love God*

(Romans 8:28 KJV)

RED

as in

Russia

and

Measles

and

Love

By
Linda Jane Niedfeldt

Cover artwork by Sara Kobs

Library of Congress Card 92-63029
Northwestern Publishing House
1250 N. 113th St., Milwaukee, Wl 53226-3284
© 1992 by Northwestern Publishing House
Published 1992
Printed in the United States of America
ISBN 0-8100-0469-0

Acknowledgements

I'd like to thank Lydia Zangl and Erica Borgen, sisters who shared the memories of their childhood with me. They surived some of the scenes described in this book.

I'd also like to thank my son, Joel, who pulled me through self-inflicted computer glitches and my friend, Denise, who gently critiqued my writing.

Chapter 1

We had only a second's warning. Papa had been giving our morning devotion, talking about the mansions of heaven. My thoughts had drifted to America. They always did when Papa talked about mansions or heaven. Then the Russian soldiers' stiff-legged marching thudded on the ground outside our school and jarred my empty stomach. Commandant Chukov slammed through the school door.

The half dozen village children and I froze on the bench against the rough wood and mud wall. Papa stood firm, his Bible tucked under his arm. His right hand lifted slightly as if to say, "Children, remain seated."

Chukov strode over to Papa, his beady eyes glaring into Papa's calm face. "Schoolmaster, Pavel Schallert," Chukov said, spitting out the words at Papa. He spoke in German so that all of us could understand. "Your teachings about God are confusing our Russian children. There is no God! And do not talk of heaven either. That is a fairy tale. Talk instead of work and improving life here in Russia. Look to the Party—the Communist Party. You German-Russian people must wake up! This is 1926. You and your teachings are obsolete and dangerous to the good of Russia. As of this hour, Schallert, you are forbidden to teach any children. Your Lutheran school is officially closed."

Closed? My school closed? I couldn't breathe. My heart seemed to jump up and pound between my ears. When Papa had read stories to us, we could escape the drab village life of Prebnow and travel in our thoughts to lovely lands. I was anxious for the day I could read to myself, but now . . . No, it can't be, I thought. How will I ever learn to read? Oh, please, God, no!

I wanted to jump up and pound Chukov with my fists. I pictured myself driving that awful man out of my school. Then I looked at Papa. His broad face, lined with hunger, did not show hatred. Instead his lips pressed in a thin, pale line. I knew he was struggling to keep angry words inside, but his face was set in that familiar "practicing patience" look.

I'd seen it often when I had grumbled about our food or had done something foolish without thinking. Then he would say, "Lisenka, you are making me practice patience again!"

Maybe all the practice I gave Papa was good because he did not argue; instead he quickly stepped back from the door as three more soldiers crowded into our tiny school.

Their faces were young, but their eyes were as cold as the axes they carried. They wore dark gray coats that hung down to their knees and tall black boots that almost reached up to touch their coats. When they snapped the heels of their boots together, we children cowered closer to the wall. Their big rough hands herded Papa and us children into the back corner. Then they shouted angrily in Russian. I could understand only snatches, like "God" and "no more."

We followed Papa's example; no one fought back. Papa gathered us into the corner and shielded us with his body.

I was trembling, but I had to see. I peeked around Papa as Chukov fired off a few words. The soldiers lifted their axes, and murderous threats hissed from their lips. For a second the axes paused in mid-air, glistening in the morning sun that streamed through the open door. Then they swung down, and I squeezed my eyes shut in terror. I expected their blows to strike down Papa, then us. The terrified screams of the other children, who shared my fateful thought, bombarded my ears. Their screams were replaced by the sound of splintering wood ripping through the room. Wood slivers flew through the air, bouncing off the walls and peppering us.

I thanked God when I realized the axes were not aimed at us. But then an equally frightening thought crossed my mind. "Oh, please, no, don't destroy my school!" I whispered, collapsing to the floor. I pulled my old cotton skirt over my knees and hugged them tight. In desperation I wound my shawl around my head to keep out the dreadful sounds, for the sound of the splintering wood also meant the splintering of my hope—my hope of ever learning to read.

It didn't take long for the soldiers to chop up the

few benches and tables in our school. When the crashing stopped and the boots snapped out the door, none of us moved. The crying continued, and my eyes would not open to look at what was left of my dear school.

I smelled a whiff of smoke. Outside a cheer erupted, and then the sound of marching feet faded down the village lane. "Papa, did they set our church-school on fire?" I asked in a panicky whisper. We'd held church and school in the same building until the Russians had forbidden our worshiping. Since then the building had just been used as a school and now . . . a sob caught in my throat. And now they might as well burn it. We have no use for a church. We have no use for a school.

"Oh, no, Lisenka," Papa answered, breaking into my thoughts. "The soldiers are burning our few books and papers. Don't fret. We will miss them, but we will adjust. We must learn to adjust."

Papa put his hand under my chin and lifted my face. "Look what they forgot to take," he said. "Look!"

I opened my stinging eyes. Papa still held his Bible in his left hand. A smile spread across his face and twinkled in his blue eyes.

"Look, children! God blinded the soldiers' eyes so that they did not even see the greatest treasure in this room. God has spared our Bible from the flames. Let's thank him. Will you pray with me?" Papa said.

The other children, tears streaking down their

hollow cheeks, looked with amazement at Papa's beaming face and then dropped to the floor beside me in a close huddle. No one had moved from the back corner, but the crying had stopped.

"Heavenly Father," Papa said softly, "at times we feel our troubles are too great to bear. We're always hungry. Cruel soldiers guard us and our village. Our church has been closed and now our school, too. But you have given us what we need—faith in your Son, our Savior. Now you have blessed us again by sparing our Bible, your Word. Thank you! Please take the anger from our hearts and replace it with love for all men, even the soldiers and Commandant Chukov. Amen."

Never, Papa, I thought. I can't love those evil men—ever. My anger simmered.

The other children began to struggle to their feet. Calm had settled on their faces, but my jaw was locked tight. My knees were flattened on the hard floor and my back was stooped. I felt old. Could I still be only ten?

I glanced at Papa. He continued to stand with bowed head and folded hands, grasping the Bible with white knuckles. He is praying for patience again, I concluded, as I slowly stood, straightening my back. Perhaps he prays for too much patience.

In hushed whispers the others tip-toed out the door. They walked slowly as if in a funeral march—the funeral of our little Lutheran school.

Now one day will be much like another, I thought. There will be no more chances to read and cipher.

No stories will add color to our drab village. No morning devotions will give us hope of heaven. We will work in brown fields and sleep in brown houses and eat brown potato peels. I scowled, remembering how Chukov and the soldiers had taken away our last bit of joy.

I hate them!

Papa spoke softly. His voice jarred the quiet. His words jarred my conscience. "Lisenka, have you found room in your heart to forgive?"

No, Papa, I thought, but I could not answer.

Chapter 2

"No soup line for you today!" Taty said to me, her thin face crinkling into a smile.

"And no watery soup dipped from a bucket for our supper!" I said, returning her smile. Several months had passed since Chukov had closed our school. The hurt was still in my heart, but I could again smile.

"Please, Senka," begged two-year-old Yurgi. "Take me with you!" His bare feet pranced merrily in front of me.

"No, child, this is an errand that Lisenka had best do alone, said Taty, jumping to my rescue. She patted the bread dough for the kraut kuchen, "Who would help me with our special supper if you went?"

Yurgi pulled back his shoulders proudly. Four-year-old Alya stood watching.

"Come, Alya," Taty said to her. "I need your help, too."

Alya smiled in her quiet way and skipped over to the table. Taty tore off two pieces of dough and handed one to each child. Their blonde, curly heads bent over the table as they began to knead their dough. Both are fragile looking like their mama, I thought, and so unlike me with my straight, brown braids, brown eyes, and broad face.

Taty began to hum softly and my eyes turned to her. Soon I would be as tall as she is, I realized.

Taty, really named Tatyana, was not my real mama. My mama had died when I was three. Papa said she'd died of starvation. Some said it was typhus. We do not know. There was no doctor. I remember my mama's warm lap and soft voice, but I can't picture her face. When I try, I only see Taty.

Dear Taty, with her callused, hard-working hands and white kerchief tied over her blonde curls, had pulled me close that day Papa had brought her home as his new bride. I was five. Her love filled the hole in my heart that had opened when they buried Mama. Taty was Mama to me now, but I still called her Taty.

Feeling my eyes on her, Taty looked up with a smile. "You have an important job to do, too. Be on your way, little lady, and don't forget the extra shawl," Taty said to me and waved her floured hand toward the door.

I grabbed the tattered shawl and swung out the wood slat door of our little house, pausing on the step. I was surprised by the bright sunshine. Our one-room house with its thatched roof and mud walls was cool in the summer and warm in the winter, but always dark. The one small window beside the door allowed in very little light and it was high, too. Only Papa was tall enough to look out.

When my eyes adjusted to the glare of the autumn sky, I started down the dusty lane that led through Prebnow to the Schmidt house. I was glad Taty had given me time alone.

Summer hadn't given me much quiet time in which to think. I'd always been with people, hoeing in the village fields with the other women or watching Alya and Yurgi while Taty worked for the village farms.

Those two little ones kept me busy—especially Yurgi. He never stopped running. It was even harder for Taty to keep up with him. She always seemed tired.

Could another baby be on the way, I wondered? Taty had been tired before Alya's birth and again before Yurgi's. A little baby would be wonderful, I thought, then stopped short. How will we have enough food for another?

My stomach gnawed on my ribs and reminded me of my errand. The boiled potato peels we'd had mid-morning did not fill me up. But supper is in only a few hours, I chided myself, and it will be special. We are having meat!

Even though Papa was no longer the school master, Herr Schmidt still remembered to share with us. He had secretly butchered an old sow and had promised Papa a sausage. I must hurry and pick it up.

As I shuffled near the locked church-school, I couldn't look at the hushed building; instead I watched the little puffs of dust float between my bare toes. The dust is powdery smooth and warm now, I thought, but before long it will become hardened with frost.

I remembered the one winter we all wore shoes sent by Americans; other years we just wrapped our feet in rags when it became very cold. I sighed. With the Communists taking so many of our supplies, this will probably be a "rag" year.

I continued down the lane and allowed myself to look around. A few small children played near their homes, but most of the men and women were in the fields, finishing up the harvest. The houses, just like ours, were all made from hardened mud; at the crossroads stood one wooden building, our little store.

Papa shopped there for flour, sugar, and lard. Once when Taty's hens laid an extra egg, she let me buy a piece of candy with the egg. We seldom paid with coins.

The candy was supposed to be a treat, but it stuck to my teeth and its thick sweetness coated my throat. I had to rush to the water bucket for a long drink.

Papa had laughed and said, "Lisenka, you are fortunate to be a little German girl living in Russia. If you were a little German girl living in America, you'd beg your mama for candy and eat it often—all the children in America like candy."

Papa had surprised me by talking about America. He seldom did.

"America!" I wonder what it would be like to live there. Papa had been there once to work and earn money. He'd planned to bring Mama and me there, too. But when Papa returned to Russia, Mama was dead, and Papa didn't talk about going to America anymore.

"Perhaps God wants us here, Lisenka," he had said

to me when I'd asked him about America. Then his shoulders had sagged and his eyes had brimmed with tears. "Perhaps, if I'd stayed here and not gone off to America chasing wild dreams, your mama would not have died."

After that I never begged to hear about America, but I listened for hints. America! I dreamed about living there. I couldn't help dreaming.

"Little girl!" someone yelled. "Where are you going?"

I looked up, surprised to hear a voice on the quiet village lane. Chukov swung out the store door, slapped the heels of his tall, black boots together, and stood, with his hands on his hips, glaring at me.

Chapter 3

"Speak up, girl! Aren't you Pavel Schallert's daughter? We missed your family in the soup line today!" Chukov said with an ugly smile.

My mind whirled! Every afternoon all summer long I'd gone to the soup line. Soldiers filled my bucket with watery, tasteless stuff which I took home for the rest. It filled our stomachs—for a while. How did Chukov notice that we skipped today? He wasn't always there. Could he suspect that the German-Russian people had had a butchering? Had I said "America" aloud? Could Chukov hear my thoughts? It seemed so. Should I run?

Instead, with my face flushed, and my voice a hollow sound in my ears, I said, "Ja, I am Herr Schallert's daughter. Taty had little work at home for me today and asked me to go to the Volga River to fish for supper. I must be hurrying. Good day, Commandant."

With a forced smile, I turned. My knees quivered like cooked cabbage, but they carried me away. Chukov did not call me back. I dared not look to see if he followed. My face burned with guilt; I knew I'd lied.

Now what should I do, I wondered in panic. If Chukov learns of the butchering, he will steal our people's meat and then explain that it's for the good of Russia. Of course, he will be generous with feeding himself first. No, I'm not giving him any idea! I'd better cut through the fields toward the river and look like I'm going fishing, I concluded.

Most of the crops had been harvested already so I could walk through the fields quickly. I remembered Papa's words as he had carefully packed our potatoes, squash, cabbages, and a few watermelons between straw in our cellar. "The Lord blessed our labors with bountiful crops this year. We, however, will have to be thrifty. Most of our crops have been shipped off to the city. City folk are hungry, too."

That was Papa—always generous and forgiving. I stomped on toward the river.

After I'd gone through several fields and was out of sight of Prebnow and Chukov's beady eyes, I cut back along a stone wall. It seemed safe to go to the Schmidts now. Darting through the tall grass in the back yards, I skirted the house and dashed into the door. Knocking took too long. I must not be seen by Chukov.

Frau Schmidt looked startled; then she bustled over to give me a squeeze. "Lisenka, welcome! I was worried you'd forgotten."

I laughed at the idea. "We'd never forget to pick up a sausage!" I whispered and handed her my shawl.

Frau Schmidt smiled, silently lifted a floor board, pulled out a large ring of sausage, and quickly wound the shawl around it.

The smell of spices mingled with meat tickled my

nose. "Oh, thank you, Frau Schmidt. We will have a wonderful supper because of you!" I hugged the sausage.

Tears glistened in her eyes. "Be on your way, child," she said, "and keep away from any soldiers."

Her warning was not necessary. I planned to stay far away. With the shawl-wrapped sausage tucked under one arm and another shawl wrapped over my shoulders to hide it, I cautiously peeked down the lane. All was clear, so I started through the village toward home.

This is going to be easy, I thought, as I neared the middle of the village. Taty will have the kraut kuchen ready. Papa will be home from the fields, and we will all soon be sitting down to a feast!

Then I heard a door slam. Chukov, his back toward me, was locking the church door. Had he seen me? I charged between two houses, ran behind a shed, and ducked into the tall weeds against the rough wall. My heart was pounding, my stomach was knotting, and the sausage was sending out tempting smells. I knew I had to do something, but I could not think.

My stomach was growling loudly.

Oh, the sausage smells so good! How can I think? Papa would want me to quiet my stomach. I will just take a little bit of the sausage—a little of my share for supper.

I took one nibble and slowly chewed. Then another. The spicy meat was delicious. I leaned back against the building and closed my eyes. Nothing had ever tasted as good as this sausage. I craved more. Hungrily, I sat up and bit off a bigger hunk. I forgot about eating only my share. I forgot about Papa and Taty, Alya and Yurgi, and our special supper. There were no thoughts in my head—only a need. Like a starving animal I tore at the sausage until it was gone.

Immediately accusing thoughts stabbed at my heart. "Oh, no," I sobbed, "how could I have been so selfish? There is none left to give Taty; little Alya and Yurgi need meat to grow, but they will have none. Papa worked so hard picking and carrying pumpkins all day. Kraut kuchen without meat will not fill his stomach. What have I done? Oh, what have I done? I'm a hateful person."

I rolled over and buried my face in the dirt and weeds.

Chapter 4

The afternoon was fading into evening when I dragged myself home. Papa must have been watching for me from the window because he rushed out the door and pulled me close.

"Lisenka, where have you been? We were so afraid Chukov or one of the soldiers had harmed you. Did anyone?" He stepped back to look at me.

"No, Papa, but I had to lie to Chukov. I was so scared, and I knew he must not find out about the butchering so I told him I was going fishing. Was that all right?"

Papa looked concerned. "Lying is not right, even if you were protecting others. God tells us to be truthful; he is strong enough to handle the rest." I trembled and blushed at Papa's scolding.

He smiled at me and then noticed the empty shawl. "Where is the sausage?" he asked.

My smile was stiff. I felt trapped. The truth was evil; lying was evil. Suddenly I blurted, "The Schmidts aren't butchering today, but I visited with Frau Schmidt. Sorry it got so late."

I'd never lied to Papa before. He held me at arms' length and studied my face. His lips formed that thin, pale line—his "practicing patience" look. Then he gave me another hug and pulled me toward the house.

"Come, Lisenka. Let's celebrate your safe return. We will not notice the sausage that is not here."

I began to wish I would not be noticing that missing sausage. It had already caused me much trouble, and now it was beginning to churn and heave in my stomach.

Just then Alya and Yurgi flew out the door. They skipped around us and then threw their arms around me—around the lump in my stomach. Next Taty appeared, giving me a side-by-side hug. It jostled my stomach more.

If they knew the truth, would they still love me? How could they? A sob started deep inside and then trembled through my body. The lump heaved again. Pulling away, I slapped my hand across my mouth and charged behind the house. I doubled over with my head in the tall grass and vomited. My stomach wrenched again and again. Finally, the lump was gone, but not my shame. I stayed doubled over, my body shaking.

Then Papa's cool hand patted my hot, quivering back; he gently pulled me straight and wiped my face with his handkerchief.

"Lisenka, Lisenka," he said softly, cradling me in his arms, "why did you lie to me? When you did not return, I visited the Schmidts. I knew they had butchered and given you the sausage. Now I know what became of it."

"Papa, I couldn't tell you the truth," I said, and

23

then told him what had happened. "I didn't mean to eat the whole sausage, Papa. It just happened."

"Eating the whole sausage was wrong, but lying to me was worse. Two wrongs never make things right! Do you understand?"

I nodded.

"God is certainly fighting for you, little lady. He loves you so much that he made you face the truth immediately. Those sins we keep secret build walls between us and God. God's not taking any chances on being locked out of your life," he said.

"I do feel better, Papa! It's good that God made me tell the truth. Lying to you was awful!"

Papa brushed the stray hair off my moist forehead.

"I'm thankful, too," Papa said, "and I understand your hunger. I'm hungry, too, but hunger for you as a child is worse. It was not like this in the old Russia. When I was a boy, before the Communists took over and we became Red Russia, we worked hard, but hard work meant enough food. Now we slave in the fields only to have the Red soldiers take most of our crops. It is not right."

I looked at Papa, surprised at the fierce anger in his voice. He was no longer talking to me. His eyes were looking far away at the setting sun.

Then Papa said, "How much longer can we stand it? Our children go hungry and uneducated. We cannot even take our burdens to the Lord at church with fellow Christians. We live in constant fear of arrest or death. How much longer? How much longer can we endure?"

There was a fire in his eyes and a hardness to his mouth. Then Papa looked at me. Tenderness washed back over his face.

"I do understand, Lisenka. I understand your hunger and your shame, but please promise me this—you'll never lie to me again. No matter what!"

"I promise, Papa!" I said. "I really promise."

"Good! Now let's go get some kraut kuchen. Taty has kept the fire going for hours, warming it. Be sure to tell her you like your crust extra brown!" he said with a chuckle.

Alya, Yurgi, and Taty were sitting on the bench, quietly waiting at the table. All six eyes were on my flushed face.

Papa broke the silence. "Taty, we are hungry. Bring on the kraut kuchen."

Nobody asked questions and soon happy chatter filled the room. The kraut kuchen did taste delicious.

"Taty," I said, remembering Papa's words, "this kraut kuchen is extra good so brown!"

Taty's eyes twinkled, but before she could answer, someone hammered on the door.

"Come in," Papa began as the door slammed open and Chukov strode in.

"Good evening, Schallert," Chukov said with a sneer. "Are you enjoying your supper tonight? Did you not wish to use the generosity of the Party? Are you tired of soup?"

None of us had moved. Then he stared wickedly at me and asked, "Are there no fish in the river, little girl? They are very slippery to catch without a pole."

I squirmed and looked at Papa. He smiled and nodded encouragement. Gulping down the bit of kuchen still in my mouth, I answered, truthfully, "No, Commandant, no fish today."

Papa then added, "Ja, Chukov, we should have been grateful for our soup again. Now look. We have only kraut kuchen. Tomorrow we will be back in the soup line."

Chukov walked slowly around the table, looking at each of us and sniffing the air. Then he slapped his heels together and marched out.

Taty quickly got up and closed the door.

"Thank you for your concern, Chukov. Good evening to you, too," Papa said to the closed door. His eyes crinkled, and we all began to giggle at his silliness.

Then Papa turned to me. His face was again serious. "When we do wrong, God is never pleased, but sometimes he will take the mess we've made and bless us anyway. Here, Lisenka, is such an example. Chukov was suspicious of a butchering, but you have destroyed the evidence. Now, I believe, he will quit looking."

I sighed with relief.

"God promises that 'all things work together for good to them that love [him],' and today he showed us that twice," Papa said.

Chapter 5

"Taty," I whispered, "what do you think Chukov and his men are building in our church-school?" It was the same question I'd asked her and Papa many times during the past months, during the gray, icy winter that had nearly passed.

No answer came, only a sigh and the sound of deep breathing from the back corner where Taty rested on her straw mattress.

Good, I thought, forgetting my question. She sleeps. She needs to sleep.

Taty fought exhaustion to take care of us. Papa was worried about her. He said that having babies was not easy for her. Taty had her baby a few weeks ago. He was born too early. He died. Taty cried often, and she hadn't yet regained her strength.

How could she, I wondered, bitterly. The watery soup from the soup line and the few vegetables from our cellar give us little strength and here we sit, shivering, with only a tiny fire in the stove. It may be spring, but the air is winter.

"Senka," Yurgi said, "help me tie this knot."

I'd forgotten Yurgi and Alya. They were sitting beside me on the floor, tying wads of straw into rough dolls. How precious Alya and Yurgi were; their little bodies stooped over and their foreheads creased as they struggled to make dolls similar to the one I'd made for them.

"Ja, Yurgi," I said, hugging him between my arms and tying his knot. Then I patted Alya on the head.

"That is good, Alya. You are able to tie your own knots now!"

She smiled proudly. Already she was very independent and eager to learn.

As the late afternoon sun filtered through our window, the question again surfaced in my mind. I wonder what Chukov and his men are building in our church-school? Could they be planning a new school for us village children?

I did not know. Papa and Taty did not either, but Papa had warned me, "Lisenka, it cannot be a school like we had. A new school will mean a new teacher, a teacher from the Communist Party, a teacher who does not believe in God. I am afraid of what a new teacher would tell you."

"Oh, Papa, don't be afraid! You can teach me about God at home, and my new teacher can teach me to read at school. It will be fine!" I had said, trying to convince Papa and maybe myself.

Papa had not looked convinced.

"In the meantime," he said, "we will continue our Bible reading lessons each night."

And we had. Each night during the few minutes of light between Papa's return from the fields and the sun's setting, Papa would help me read the Bible. But I felt so very slow.

The door rattled and Papa walked in. He quietly shut the door and slumped against it. Alya and Yurgi began to leap in their usual excitement at seeing Papa and then froze on the floor. Papa's face shone with love for us . . . and with sorrow . . . and with something else.

"Lisenka, there will be no school for you this next year either," Papa said.

I knew in that second that he spoke the truth, but I wanted to scream, "No, you are teasing me, Papa." I could not say that. I could not even ask, "Why?" A sob trapped all my words.

Papa continued, "Chukov and his men are rebuilding our church-school to be a museum—a museum of atheism."

Papa shuddered. His smooth shaven face looked old, matching the gray tone of his tattered jacket.

"It is happening all over Russia," Papa said. "The cross of our Savior is being replaced with statues of Lenin. Churches are being turned into places to dishonor God and honor the Communist Party, places where they can lie to us with promises of 'bread, land, and peace.'"

That "something else" shown in his eyes again—a fire. I quickly caught sight of the flame and exclaimed, "How can they use God's house in such a way? When will they stop mocking God and . . . hurting us?"

Papa shook his head, closed his eyes, and gave me

no answer.

My anger simmered, then exploded, "How can they take away my school?"

Papa's lips tightened, and he gave me no answer.

I sprung up and raced to him. Grabbing his arm, I begged, "Answer me, Papa. Where are the answers?"

Finally Papa opened his eyes and said carefully, "Some questions we can answer now, some later, and some answers we will not find in this world, but God answers every necessary question in his Word. Let's turn to it now. Do you think we have time to get to our reading lesson before dark?"

The fire was gone from his eyes. He said, "Now more than ever you must continue to practice reading."

He smiled with tight lips.

My mind screamed, "Papa, we must fight back," but my voice said, "Ja, Papa," and I pulled the Bible from its hiding place under the bench.

Alya and Yurgi still had not moved. With big eyes they'd been watching Papa and me. At least, I've had a chance to go to school and begin to read, I thought. What will become of these little ones?

Just then Papa swooped down on Alya and Yurgi, scooped them up, one under each arm, and twirled around until their giggles filled the room. Even Taty, who had awakened and had been quietly watching from her mattress, chuckled. I could not join their merriment. Papa was being silly for the sake of the little ones. Life was not happy. He did not fool me.

"Papa, I am ready. The light is fading so we better hurry," I said, deliberately cutting into the fun.

Quickly I opened the Bible to the book of Ezekiel. Papa sat down beside me on the bench, wrapped one arm around me, and pulled me close.

"Look at this, Lisenka," he said. "You're already in chapter forty-five. Go ahead; begin reading at verse nine."

I began confidently, "'This is what the . . . the S - S - S.' Oh, Papa, I am so very slow!"

"Nonsense. That's a very difficult word. It's *sovereign* and means above all others. There, now keep going."

I began again, " 'This is what the S-s-sovereign LORD says: You have gone far e-enough, O princes of Israel! Give up your v-vi-.'"

"Violence," prompted Papa. "Violence and oppression."

"'Give up your violence and oppression,'" I read, "'And do what is just and right. Stop dis . . . poss . . . essing . . . dispossessing my people.' How's that?"

Papa did not praise me as usual. When I glanced up, his eyes were staring at the page. Then he slowly looked at me but did not focus on my face. The fire had returned. He repeated the words—not to me, but to himself—"You have gone far enough."

Then his voice rose as he seemed to be commanding someone unseen, "'Give up your violence and oppression and do what is right. Stop dispossessing my people.'" Papa's voice became a shout, "'Declares the Sovereign LORD.'"

Taty hurried to Papa, gently covering his lips with her hand. "Pavel," she said, "please, someone will hear you."

Papa pulled Taty down on the bench beside him. "Tatyana," he demanded, "how can we continue to live under a government which mocks the Lord and oppresses us, his people?"

"But we still have our Bible," Taty replied. "And we still have each other and the children. You can teach the children God's truths, and you can teach them to read, too. What else can we do? I'm too afraid to think about it." Taty choked on the last words and shoved her knuckles into her mouth.

A shadow flickered across the window, and a second later the door flew open. Chukov and two soldiers strode into the dark room. My hands tried to hide the Bible behind me, but it was too late. Chukov swaggered over to me and snapped his hand out. Papa's arm had turned to steel behind me, but his voice remained calm.

"Lisenka, give Chukov the book."

I glared at Chukov, my eyes mirroring his hatred, and I could not move. I could not willingly give this evil man my last glimmer of hope.

Chukov snatched the Bible from my grasp and shook it in Papa's face. "Schallert, for such a learned man, your ignorance is amazing. For lesser disobedience men have disappeared forever. If you want to stay with your precious family, obey the rules. There is no God. Do not teach your family lies. There will be no more warnings," Chukov hissed. Then he clicked his heels together and strutted from the house with his two men following like puppets.

The room was deathly quiet. Taty and the little ones began to cry. Papa pulled us all to him, but he could not fill the emptiness.

Chapter 6

That night, as handfuls of twisted straw burned in the deep metal tub we used for a stove, Papa played his violin. He played the hymn he often played, but this time he warned us, "Let your hearts sing 'A Mighty Fortress Is Our God,' but keep your voices silent . . . for a little while your voices must be silent."

Soon the soft glow from the stove and the gentle music lulled Alya and Yurgi to sleep. They snored beside me on our straw mattress on the floor. Taty, overcome with exhaustion, drifted off too, but my mind could not rest. My body was stiff as I recalled everything that had happened. Trying to make sense of the day, I found myself questioning God's wisdom.

It had been a year ago that God had given us comfort by sparing our Bible from Chukov's fire. Now, when God's Word was all we had left, God allowed the Bible to be snatched from us. How could that be for our good?

The fire was dying down, but I could faintly see Papa's face. It looked calm. He seemed to be singing with his heart as he played another hymn.

Papa loved to sing praises to God with gusto. I wondered when we'd hear his voice again.

Then I said aloud, "How long will your voice have to be silent? What did you mean by 'for a little while our voices must be silent'? How long is 'a little while'?"

Papa continued to play, but glanced at me briefly—just long enough for me to see his eyes. Had the fire returned?

I scurried over to the bench where he sat and studied him from my perch on the floor.

Ja, his eyes were smoldering, but his lips were smiling.

"Lisenka, how you remind me of your mama. Her eyes were dark, and she had dark braided hair and rosy cheeks, too. She could read my face and know my thoughts. Tell me, what am I thinking?" Papa asked teasingly.

My elbows rested on Papa's knees; I looked at him, and I thought. I wanted to read his mind as my mama once did, but for now I had to admit, "Papa, I cannot tell your thoughts. Tell me, please."

"Lisenka, I know how disappointed you are that there will be no school for you. Now even our textbook, our precious Bible, is gone, and we cannot even practice reading."

I gulped. The promises of tomorrow . . . and the next day . . . and the next day were gone. Only a drab gloom hung on the horizon.

Papa continued, "I worried about your lack of education and that of little Alya and Yurgi, but I knew we could teach you enough at home to get by. Now, however, my thoughts have changed."

"I know, Papa. I can see it in your eyes. What are your thoughts?" I begged.

Papa's music continued, louder than his words. Nobody outside our door could have heard him. Still he spoke more softly. "Chukov has now taken our 'one thing needful.' We have God in our hearts, but without the daily study of his Word, I'm afraid our faith may falter. If we gather with our fellow believers to worship the Lord, we must live in fear of discovery, fear of imprisonment, and even fear of death. I cannot live this way. I will not."

Exasperated, I asked once more, "What will we do, Papa? What are you thinking?"

Papa studied my eager face, then shook his head. "No, no, Lisenka. I cannot tell you. It is too dangerous for you to know. If you do not know, you will not have to worry about keeping it secret."

A secret! My mind whirled. What kind of secret would give Papa a quiet fire in his eyes?

Once more I looked at Papa and searched my mind. Suddenly, I knew. As my mama did long ago, I looked at Papa, and I just knew.

"We are going to America!" I stated confidently. "Am I right, Papa?"

Chapter 7

"All things," I said, as I rolled the ball of bread dough over, "work together." I continued—sprinkling flour on the rough wooden table and kneading the dough—"for [our] good." I gave the dough one final pat and then began to press it into a thin circle. "All things work together for [our] good," I repeated as I sprinkled chopped cabbage and onions onto the dough.

Ever since Papa told me about his plans to take us to America, I had renewed confidence in God's wisdom. If our church and school had not been closed, if our Bible had not been taken, if Chukov had not threatened Papa . . . then perhaps we'd have been content to stay in this drab village and just exist. But God had allowed all those things to happen, and now Papa's dream, the dream that had died with Mama, was again alive. We were going to America! The thought sent a shiver of pleasure down my spine. Ja, "all things do work together for good to them that love God."

I turned back to my baking, folding the dough in half and pinching the edges together. There! A kraut kuchen made all by myself. Wouldn't Taty and Papa be proud of me? When they returned from the fields, I'd have supper all ready.

I held my arm over the tub-stove. The fire in the bottom seemed hot enough so I gently placed the kraut kuchen in a heavy kettle and lowered it into the stove to bake.

America, I thought again. How much longer will I be able to wait?

Papa had said, "We must work hard to produce a good crop this year for Chukov and the other Reds. Then when the vegetables are shipped off and our little supply is stored in the cellar, we will slip away. Before Chukov and the others realize it, we will be gone."

I remembered saying, "Papa, how can I wait that long?"

Papa's face had become stern, his lips pressed in that thin, pale line. "Lisenka, you must be patient," he warned. "You must act as if we will be spending another winter here. If you act differently and arouse suspicion, our escape will be blocked and perhaps . . . "

He did not continue. I knew what could happen. Practicing patience was a necessity. I had to do it. Our lives depended on it.

With the kraut kuchen baking slowly in the stove, I stepped outside to check on Alya and Yurgi. Alya loved watching Yurgi and kept her eyes on him like a mother hen. Yurgi, now that he was three, was spunky, but could be trusted not to run off.

I squinted down the dusty lane.

"Yurgi! Alya!" I called. No answer.

I trotted around the house. Alya sat there in the tall grass, making dandelion chains. So deep was her concentration that she did not hear me coming.

"Where is Yurgi?" I asked urgently.

Alya's hands flew to her face. Fear swept over her. She had forgotten about Yurgi for a few minutes.

Suddenly from the chicken coop came a loud s-q-u-a-w-k and a wild rush of wings. A horrifying scream followed.

My hair bristled on the back of my neck and a cold surge overpowered me. That was Yurgi's scream. For a seemingly endless moment my feet stayed put, as if they were weighted down with spring mud. Then they released me, and I rushed forward.

Chickens crashed and fluttered as I charged through the doorway of the coop. My eyes darted about, trying to adjust to the darkness and see through the thick dust. Finally I saw Yurgi, sitting on the dirt floor, glaring at our rooster with a challenging look. The rooster was much bigger than any of our hens and always carried himself with pride. Now he strutted proudly around Yurgi, returning his challenge.

Immediately, I realized both the rooster and Yurgi were cocked and ready to fight again and that I was the only person who could stop their foolishness. I grabbed a stick to hold off the rooster, and with the other hand I dragged Yurgi out the door.

"That chicken attacked me, Senka," Yurgi screamed. "Let me get her."

I smiled down at the struggling little boy. Alya ran up to give him a hug and then gasped, "Yurgi, you have blood running down your face!"

Yurgi quickly wiped his forehead and then stared at his hand. "That chicken hurt me, Senka," he said with a sob. "And all I wanted to do was get the eggs."

When I parted Yurgi's hair, I saw two peck marks with blood seeping from them. My insides quivered, but I managed to say rather calmly, "Come, Yurgi, We need to take care of your battle wounds. You're a brave little boy not to cry."

I knew if I acted calmly, it would relax Yurgi. Papa had often used the same trick on me. Yurgi obediently took my hand. Alya too quit jumping around in panic and quietly followed.

"Alya, you sit here with Yurgi," I commanded, pointing to the wooden bench outside the door.

Quickly Alya sat, pulling Yurgi onto her lap. Both of them now had tears streaming down their faces. I knelt in front of them, fighting my own tears.

"Senka will make it better," I said, looking at Yurgi. Then I added to Alya, "It's all right. I left you too long in charge of Yurgi. It was my fault."

As soon as Alya began to smile through her glistening tears, I darted inside. Then my own tears began.

Poor Yurgi. What if that rooster had pecked his eyes. Poor Alya. She feels responsible for what happened when it was really my fault for day-dreaming over that kuchen.

Will Papa and Taty ever trust me again? More hot tears ran down my face before I could shake off the self-pity.

Yurgi needs my attention now. Grabbing a tin mug, I dipped it into the water bucket. Silently I thanked Papa for always making sure we had clean water from the village well. Next I pulled a bottle of iodine off the shelf and took one of Taty's clean kerchiefs from her wooden peg on the wall.

Outside Alya still sat cradling Yurgi.

Yurgi was quiet, trusting me, while I washed the wounds and then dabbed them with iodine. When I tied Taty's kerchief around his head, I explained, "This will keep the wounds clean." Then I looked at his sweet, little face and added, "Until we take Mama's kerchief off, we will have to call you Yurgiana."

Both little ones giggled. I smiled with relief. The crisis was over.

That evening at supper Alya and Yurgi took turns chattering to Papa and Taty about their adventure and giggling over Yurgi's new name.

"Don't forget, Papa," Yurgi giggled, "my name is Yurgiana."

My conscience bothered me, however, so I quietly picked at my kraut kuchen, keeping my eyes on my tin bowl. The kraut kuchen I'd been so proud to serve seemed tasteless now.

I could feel Taty's eyes resting on me.

"Lisenka," she said quietly, "Do not feel badly. I often allow the children to play outdoors alone while I prepare supper."

Papa smiled at me and added, "You acted very grown up in caring for Yurgi, and your kraut kuchen is as good as Taty's."

They still trusted me! I smiled.

"Ja, don't blame yourself," Taty said. "Many times we have warned Yurgi to stay out of that chicken coop."

Yurgi piped up, "But, Mama, I was only trying to gather eggs from under that big, red chicken."

Papa's head tipped backwards, and his stomach began to shake in a deep laugh. We all stopped and stared at him. Papa managed to sputter, "Yurgi! Yurgi!" and then burst into another peal of laughter.

"What, Papa?" Yurgi asked, looking innocent and sweet in the white kerchief.

"Yurgi," Papa said, still gasping for breath, "you must begin to spend less time with all these females. Not only do they have you dressing like a lady, they haven't bothered to explain to you that roosters don't lay eggs!"

Warm laughter erupted around the table. Only little Yurgi still looked puzzled.

Chapter 8

Spider webs stretched across the brown stems of pumpkin vines as Papa and I trudged through the empty field. Most of the crops had now been harvested. Scattered here and there were only a few green pumpkins, still clinging desperately to their stems.

"Papa," I said, my voice quivering, "do you think these little green pumpkins look sad?"

Papa stopped short and looked at me. His thoughts, I knew, had been on our escape. He often was deep in thought these days, planning again and again every detail. Our time for leaving was very near, but only Papa knew for sure the day.

Perhaps he had asked me to take this late-afternoon walk with him because he wanted me to remember clearly this land, my home since birth . . . and his, too. Perhaps it was our last walk together— ever. If we were caught escaping . . .

"What did you say, Lisenka? I am sorry; I was not listening," Papa said and waited patiently for me to speak again.

"Do you think these little green pumpkins look sad?"

"Sad? Ja, I suppose they do," he answered. "What makes them look sad to you, Lisenka?"

"Look how each one is so tiny and all alone in this big field," I began. "And how they still hold onto the mother vine in hopes of growing . . . but there is no hope for them. Soon they will die."

I said the last words in a rush. My voice was giving out. Tears filled my eyes. I was sad, yet I could not understand why.

Papa pulled me against him. His ragged, wool jacket felt warm on my cheek. His hands gently stroked my braids and then pushed the stray hairs back from my face. Neither of us moved.

Finally, I could again speak, "Papa, these lonely little pumpkins remind me of the people in our village. They live such lonely lives and cling to hopes of a better time to come. But what can Russia offer them? What will happen to them?"

"Sometimes, Lisenka, your thinking goes very deep. You are right. The people who hang onto life here do have their hopes clinging to dead vines. A Russia without God is without hope."

"What about our dreams?" I asked, finally beginning to understand my sadness. "Are we clinging to different dead vines? Will life really be better in America? I am confused . . . and afraid."

"So many questions you have in your little head today. No wonder your face is creased with worry!" Papa said, stepping back and smiling at me. He kicked a dead vine and then continued, "My dream does not grow from a dead vine. We are going to America so that I can teach you and the little ones about God. There we can all worship without fear. With our resurrected Savior as our vine, how can our dreams die? Does that make sense to you?"

Slowly I realized Papa's dreams differed from mine. I wanted to go to America to learn to read, to have enough meat to eat, to escape fear. Papa had a higher goal—to seek the Lord.

A verse Papa often repeated came to my mind. "Remember that Bible passage, Papa, 'Seek ye first the kingdom of God, and his righteousness; and all these things shall be added unto you'?"

Papa nodded.

"You really believe that, don't you, Papa?"

He nodded again.

"I believe," Papa said, "that when God has first place in our hearts, he will provide us with what we need for our day to day lives."

Papa grinned with confidence and patted my head. Slowly the corners of my mouth turned up.

"Me, too," I said, returning a big smile.

The fear and confusion left my heart.

"Lisenka, I am glad we could clear our hearts like this, but I also have a special request. I brought you out here so we could talk in private," Papa said. He glanced about the empty field. An earnestness had returned to his voice. The smile was gone.

"Everything is set," he said. "We will be leaving tomorrow night!"

My heart did a flip in my chest. "Tomorrow night?" I gasped. "So soon?" I'd practiced patience well, always thinking the time for our escape was still far off. My brain was numb. "Tomorrow night?" I repeated and shook my head. It did not seem real.

Papa chuckled at my surprise, then became serious again. "Ja, Lisenka, tomorrow night! A messenger came through the field today and gave me the word. The oxen cart will stop briefly outside Prebnow, and we must be ready to slip quietly aboard."

"I will be, Papa. How can I help?"

"I have a special errand for you to run tomorrow morning. It's urgent, but you must look as if you're just out for a morning stroll."

Papa knew how hard it was for me to be about urgent business and still look calm, but he trusted me to do it . . . and I would!

"Where will I go?" I asked.

"You will go to Herr Schmidt's house to warn them. If I went, their danger would be greater. Chukov keeps a close eye on me."

At my perplexed look, Papa continued, "Let me explain. The Schmidts are richer than most of the villagers. The Russian leaders call such rich peasants Kulaks. Many Kulaks in the surrounding areas are destroying their crops and animals in protest. The Kulaks are saying, 'We will not work hard to raise food and then have the Reds ship it away from us. If we cannot have it, nobody will.'"

"The Schmidts are not doing that, are they?" I asked.

"No, they are trying to cooperate, just as we have, but now I'm afraid it will do them no good."

"Why?" I asked.

"You can imagine that the Reds are furious with

the Kulaks who are destroying crops and animals. Now the soldiers are striking back. I have heard that the Red soldiers have driven many Kulaks from their homes."

"Where are they taken?" I asked, not believing my ears.

"They are forced to go far away to work. Sometimes whole families are taken. Sometimes just the men. Those who resist are killed."

"But what about the Schmidts?" I asked. "They're innocent." None of this made sense to me. Who would want to drive the Schmidts away?

"The Reds are looking to avoid trouble in our village before it starts. They will choose a Kulak family here and punish them as an example. They figure that will make the rest of us too afraid to do anything but cooperate."

I stood in the empty field, feeling empty inside.

Papa continued, "The messenger asked me to warn the Kulaks around here, and I will send word to the others, but Chukov's hatred for the Schmidts is powerful. Not only is Herr Schmidt richer than the rest of us, but he also is a believer. I think Chukov will choose Herr Schmidt to punish as a warning to the Kulaks . . . and a warning to us Christians."

I shuddered at such hatred. It seemed we should not wait a second longer to rush to Schmidts' house.

"How do you know that tomorrow will be soon enough?" I asked.

"The messenger thought these soldiers would not come to our village for a few days. We don't want to rush around, looking suspicious. Let's hope and pray the messenger is right."

"Ja. But where can the Schmidts go to be safe?" I asked.

"Well, Lisenka, where do you think?" Papa responded, smiling.

That smile told me the answer.

"To America?" I whispered.

"Ja, of course. Secretly, I have discussed our plans with Herr Schmidt several times. He was always undecided."

"And now, Papa?"

"And now he and his wife will be eager to join us. Don't you agree?"

"Ja, Papa," I said, relaxing.

"Good, then tomorrow morning can you take them a warning and an invitation to America?" Papa asked.

I took a deep breath, nodded, and said, "I can do that Papa . . . and I can do it right!"

Chapter 9

I carefully wrapped six eggs in my shawl to deliver to Schmidts. I was anxious to get my errand underway. Alya and Yurgi scampered around me.

"I want to come along," Alya said.

"Me, too," chimed in Yurgi.

Taty looked up from the mound of extra bread dough she was kneading to bake for our journey and said, "No, just Lisenka will go today."

Then she turned to me, her face rosy from working the dough, "Please, be careful, Lisenka."

Her smile was full of motherly love, but her eyes were sad.

"Oh, Taty," I said, "I will be fine . . . and we will be fine."

Taty answered, "I know, dear; I just can't help being a little sad to leave my home . . . and a little afraid of where we will be tomorrow . . . and next week . . . and next month."

Her voice trailed off.

I threw my arms around her neck and squeezed her tight. "We will be fine," I repeated, kissing her cheek. "Now I better be off to Schmidts'."

I stepped out our door into a burst of sunlight. Across my mind flashed my errand to Schmidts' a year ago. It had been a fall day similar to this. How dark the day had turned. How I'd messed up that errand! Well, this time would be different. I'd promised Papa.

As an added precaution, I paused and silently prayed, "Lord, be with me and keep me doing what is right today!" Reassured of God's presence, I began my stroll down the dusty lane.

These extra eggs from Taty's chickens were to share with the Schmidts. I carefully moved them to my other arm, keeping the wrap tight. Papa had come up with a good reason for my visit. Now if I met Chukov, I could look him in the eyes and without lying tell him where I was going and why!

The road ahead looked empty. Too bad! I was ready to meet Chukov and he was nowhere to be seen. I smiled to myself, knowing Papa would say I was getting too cocky.

My eyes jumped about, looking for the last time at the tiny, wood and mud houses. They were scattered along the lane, one looking much like the next. At the intersection of lanes, I deliberately kept my eyes fastened on the wooden store. I couldn't look at our church-school. Seeing it still hurt. The store was very quiet . . . so were the houses. Everything was quiet . . . too quiet. Fear muscled its way into my thoughts. I had to lick my dry lips.

What could be wrong? Where were the store customers? Where were the children who usually scampered in the lane? Where were their mamas who worked in the yards washing clothes or making soap?

Could they all be inside on such a lovely day?

Dread filled my heart—for what I did not know. I wondered whether I had the strength to do Papa's errand, but I forced my feet to keep walking. Only a few more houses and I'd be safe inside Schmidts' warm house with Frau Schmidt bustling over to give me a hug.

I began to walk faster, still carefully balancing the eggs. I had to get to Schmidts' house! Only a few steps now and . . . I stopped abruptly.

Their door hung open. Nobody stood in the doorway.

Drawing in my breath, I walked up and peeked inside. The room Frau Schmidt always kept so neat was strewn with broken furniture. The table lay lopsided with two legs sticking out awkwardly. The stove was ripped off its stand and black ashes dusted the floor. Broken benches were scattered about.

Tears began to fill my eyes. The room became a blur.

"This can't be true," I whispered, collapsing to my knees. "No! I can't be too late to warn the Schmidts. How can we be too late? Papa said we had time."

One by one the eggs rolled from the wrap and cracked on the steps. I did not care. The eggs were not important anymore.

How long did I sit there? Time had stopped.

From the back of the room came a sound—the sound of soft sobbing. "Frau Schmidt!" I called, "Is that you?"

Silence.

Quickly, carefully, I picked my way through the debris, afraid of what I would find, but determined to face whatever it was.

Frau Schmidt sat cowering in the corner behind the table. Tears and dirt streaked her face. Her eyes were blank.

"Frau Schmidt," I said softly and touched her shoulder.

She pulled back from me in fear and then relaxed when she recognized me.

"Lisenka, dear girl," she sobbed. "Are they gone now?"

"I am alone, Frau Schmidt. You are safe now. Who did this to you?" I asked, knowing the answer even before she replied.

"Soldiers came with Chukov. They told lies about my husband. With their swords they wrecked our home and forced him to go along with them. I do not know where they have taken him or when I will ever see him again."

Sobs of despair shook her entire body, and she buried her face in her hands. I pulled her close and held her tight until she stopped shaking. There were no words I could offer in comfort. I just wanted to be with her.

It took some time before I felt I could share with her my reason for coming. Even though I knew it was too late for Herr Schmidt, perhaps it was not too late for her. Papa said that Kulaks never came back.

"Tonight, Frau Schmidt, we will be leaving

Prebnow to go to America. Papa, Taty, the two little ones, and me. It is not safe for you to stay here. Will you join us?"

"What is there for me in America? I cannot leave here without my husband. The Russian soldiers will certainly realize he is innocent and send him home to me. Then, perhaps, we will think about coming to your America," she said, courageously.

I looked at her lonely smile, saw hope where there was no hope, and remembered the little green pumpkins in the dying field.

Chapter 10

We had been wrapped in darkness for hours. No light filtered through our window; no sound, except that of Alya's and Yurgi's deep breathing interrupted the quiet. My bundle—a sheet tied around two loaves of bread, a kerchief, and an extra shawl—rested against my legs. I held Alya's and Yurgi's smaller bundles on my lap, ready to hand them to the little ones the moment we roused them. Taty sat beside me on the bench, waiting too, holding hers and Papa's bundles . . . and Papa's violin, wrapped carefully in canvas. We had to travel light, but Papa's violin held many wonderful memories, and we had to have it with us.

Finally, I could not stand the waiting.

"Taty," I demanded in an urgent whisper, "we must go looking for Papa. Surely he has been arrested or worse; the oxen cart has probably come and gone."

But before Taty could answer, the door quietly swung open and Papa slipped in. "It is time!" he said to us and stooped down to gently shake Alya and Yurgi.

"Shhhh, quiet," he said as the little ones began to stir and stretch. Lifting Yurgi to his shoulders, Papa straightened, grabbed his bundle and violin, and opened the door. There he stood, waiting.

"Ja, it is time!" I said, but did not budge. Papa had moved so quickly I could not think. Taty hastened to take Alya's bundle and tenderly guided her out the door.

"Ja, it is time," Papa said again. "Are you joining us, Lisenka, or do want to wait for the next cart?"

I could hear the smile in his voice.

"Oh, Papa, is it really time?" I asked. "Are we really leaving for America?" It was still a dream. Could this be happening?

"Ja, little one, it is really time! Now you walk behind me. Taty and Alya will follow you. We must all be silent."

Papa's warning was not meant to scare us, but I caught the fear in his voice. My heart began to beat loudly, but I quickly followed him, clutching the two bundles to my chest. I would be quiet.

Outside, the stars gave enough light for me to turn and see our little house. Taty, too, hesitated and turned back for one last look. When she turned forward to follow me and Papa, I saw tears glistening on her cheeks. Ja, leaving all this behind was hardest on her.

Papa led us to the crossroads. I knew we stayed in the soft dust of the lane because our footsteps were muffled. Papa chose the route he felt was the least dangerous. We turned right, away from our church-school, without a backward glance. New religious freedom lay ahead. Soon we were nearing the edge of our village and I began to breathe more freely. The oxen cart awaited us just over the next rise.

Suddenly, cutting through the silence like a knife, came a voice, "Schallert! Where-are-you-r-r-running?"

The voice was Chukov's, yet the words were spoken differently, run together, slurred.

Papa froze, then turned slowly around. Chukov swaggered past Taty, Alya, and me to glare closely into Papa's eyes. He swayed slightly and blinked several times, trying to see Papa. The smell of liquor hung heavy in the air around him.

Papa did not speak. His eyes were closed, and his hands were poised at his side, clenched into fists. Would Papa fight, or would we turn meekly back? Would Papa be taken like Herr Schmidt, never to return to us? My thoughts flew in panicky wisps.

Chukov swayed more; slowly his knees buckled, and he fell in the dirt at the side of the lane. He lay there in a heap like a discarded straw doll. The side of his face was flattened as he lay in the dust. Saliva began to drool from his open mouth.

"Papa, what has happened to Chukov?" I exclaimed, forgetting to whisper.

Papa looked up, startled, and then whispered, "The Lord be praised! Chukov has passed out. Many other nights he has had too much to drink, but tonight he has done a great job of it. By the time he comes to, we will be hours away."

"Will he die, Papa?"

"Die? No, he will wake up in a few hours, I think, but if he continues to drink like this, it will kill him," Papa answered.

"Why does he do it?" I asked.

"Perhaps the liquor helps him forget his evil ways. Tonight, especially, after what he did to Herr Schmidt, his conscience must have bothered him. Chukov has no God; he cannot ask forgiveness . . . so he drinks to forget."

I stared for a second longer at Chukov, that pitiful man lying face down in the dust. I no longer hated him. Like Frau Schmidt he had hope in a Russia which had no hope, but much worse, he had no God.

"Hurry, Lisenka," Papa urged. "God has given us the escape. Let's use our time wisely."

Quickly, I stepped in behind Papa. Yurgi snored on Papa's shoulders. The excitement had not disturbed him. Taty and Alya followed silently behind me.

In a short time, Papa exclaimed, "Here we are!"

Quickly, he handed Yurgi to a stranger on the cart. Next he lifted Alya up.

I heard a rustling behind me and turned to see Taty running back toward the village. Near the top of the rise she stopped. My eyes strained to see. Was there someone with her?

Papa hurried after her, then stopped midway, waiting. I ran up to Papa to see. Taty and Frau Schmidt stood a few feet beyond in a farewell embrace.

"I have been waiting for you. I could not have you go without a final good-bye, dear friends. May God bless you in your new life," Frau Schmidt said to Taty.

Taty's body heaved with sobs. She could not answer.

I ran up to them and threw my arms around them

both.

"Frau Schmidt, please join us," I begged.

"No, no, dear child, that is impossible until Herr Schmidt returns," she said, "But watch for us. We will come."

Her brave words gave Taty strength.

"God bless you, too, dear friend," Taty whispered. "We will keep you in our prayers."

Papa joined us, gave Frau Schmidt a hug, and then gently pulled Taty toward the cart. "We must go now, Taty. Farewell, Frau Schmidt. Keep the faith!"

Frau Schmidt stood there in the shadows waving to us until the oxen cart had carried us over the next rise.

"Papa," I said, as she disappeared from sight, "today I thought Frau Schmidt was a little, green pumpkin with no hope, but now I'm not sure. Do you think she and Herr Schmidt will be able to join us in America?"

Papa answered, "Frau Schmidt has strong faith in God's ability to perform the impossible. She knows well the passage 'with God all things are possible,'" Papa explained.

"So Papa, do you expect to someday see them in America?"

"I cannot predict God's will, but it is possible . . . very possible," he answered.

"It is possible," I repeated to myself. "With God all things are possible . . . the Schmidts may yet escape . . . it's possible."

Sleep slowly turned my thoughts to dreams, content dreams for "with God all things are possible."

Chapter 11

I peered into the darkness and snuggled deeper into the straw, sleepily wondering why my nose was so cold. Papa better start the stove fire, I thought, as I started to drift into a deeper sleep. Suddenly my bed pitched sideways, rolling me over. My eyes flew open; immediately alert, I found myself nose to nose with a strange, snoring face. The snores sputtered, and the man began to stir. I tried frantically to turn away only to face another stranger.

Where am I? My body stiffened in panic. Then slowly I recognized the steady clop-clop noise of the oxen hooves and remembered they were carrying us to freedom. We are traveling through the night, I thought, and the cart wheel must have rolled over a rut in the road.

I relaxed again, knowing Papa, Taty, Alya, and Yurgi were also somewhere on the oxen cart, wedged between strangers, too. Last night as Papa squeezed us onto the cart, I'd whispered, "Papa, how will we all fit?"

He'd explained that there were many peasants, like us, fleeing Russia, and there were others who were risking their lives to help all of us. They needed to fill each oxen cart with as many people as possible because they never knew when the escape routes would be discovered and blocked by soldiers.

"It will be crowded," Papa had said, "But more bodies will keep you warmer."

Ja, Papa, I thought, pulling the blanket over my cold nose, I am glad for many bodies now.

The gentle sway of the oxen cart soon rocked me back to sleep again.

Not until the sun was high and its brightness had warmed the straw did I again awaken. I squinted to open my eyes. The eyes of the stranger next to me crinkled into a thousand wrinkles, and the man grinned, saying, "Guten Tag, Fraulein. Welcome aboard."

After rolling into the gentleman during the night, I felt like I already knew him. My usual shyness disappeared and I responded, "Good day to you." I smiled at the friendly face.

"My name is Gerhardt," he said, offering his hand.

"I'm Lisenka."

His handshake was iron-strong, but friendly. He continued, "My son, Johannes, is leading the oxen awhile to let me rest."

I stretched to see over the front of the cart. A boy, not much older than I, was walking beside the oxen. Even though the animals were much bigger than he was, Johannes was in control. While I watched, he commanded the oxen, "Gee," and turned us off the main road toward a grove of trees.

"Looks like breakfast time," said Gerhardt. "Would you like sausages, eggs, and biscuits this morning?

Did your mama pack such a feast?"

His eyes twinkled at his teasing, and I giggled, but my stomach did growl at the thought. Taty had packed us bread, boiled eggs, and some vegetables. That would be fine for today, but some day in America . . . maybe . . . I would have a feast for breakfast.

The cart rumbled under the canopy of the trees so travelers along the road would not notice us in the shadows. Gerhardt jumped over the side to help Johannes unhitch the oxen.

Just then the sound of horses' hooves thudded on the dirt road behind us. We all froze in silent fear. Riders, dressed in soldiers' uniforms, charged past; none even glanced in our direction.

One by one the dozen passengers relaxed and began to untangle themselves from the arms and legs of the others. But a shiver crept up my spine. Could Chukov have sent a search party after us? I shook my head to block the thought. No, we are free now, I thought, trying to reassure myself.

I spied Papa near the back, pulling Yurgi to a sitting position. Yurgi yawned and looked around, then rubbed his eyes.

I smiled to myself. Poor little Yurgi must be confused. He falls asleep in his straw mattress at home and wakes up on an oxen cart!

Then I looked across the cart and caught Taty's eyes resting quietly on me. Alya was curled up under her arm, beginning to stretch.

Taty smiled first. I grinned back. Good! She is

ready for the adventure now, I thought.

Papa struggled through the straw, dragging a giggling Yurgi under one arm. They fell into the straw beside Taty. Papa planted a kiss on Taty's cheek, then picked up a handful of straw and tossed it in my direction.

"We have escaped Chukov and those who watch us!" he said with glee. "America, we are one step closer to you!"

Papa's excitement replaced my doubts. I piled on top of him, laughing. "America, here we come!" I said.

What relief we all felt as we crawled off the cart to stretch. America seemed so very close. I wonder how many steps we yet have to go?

Chapter 12

For several days the sky had been gray and drippy. Our joy of that first morning had soon been dampened. It was hard to be joyful when we were wet, hungry, cramped, and tired. We stopped occasionally to stretch and change oxen, but the rests didn't last long. From day to night to day again we plodded along, jostled from side to side in the cart.

Papa often thanked the Lord that it hadn't rained hard, but I did not feel so thankful. The blankets over us were cold. The straw we nestled in was smelling musty. My clothes clung to my body and my braids hung limp.

We had taken many steps now, I thought glumly, and America does not seem any closer.

"Lisenka," Papa said, interrupting my thoughts, "a scowl is not becoming on such a pretty, young lady!" He winked at me from across the wagon.

I smiled, sorry for my self-pity. Papa was trying hard to keep us all happy.

I looked at Alya and Yurgi, tucked in under Papa's arms. They had whimpered for a few days, but now they rode along quietly with blank faces.

Taty moved beside me. I looked at her pale, sleeping face and remembered hearing her cough during the night. This damp air is not good for her. Quickly I pulled her blanket back under her chin, tucking it around her shoulders. A slight smile swept across her sleeping face.

Johannes, sitting next to me on the other side, suddenly spoke, "Someday I will have a daughter as pretty and gentle as you!"

My face warmed. I did not know he'd been watching me.

Johannes, my new friend, chuckled. He loved to tease me. It always brought quick color to my cheeks. He said my rosy face warmed each day. His friendship warmed me now.

I had not had such a friend for some time. After the Reds had come to our village, fear of the soldiers kept us children close to our homes. We did not have time for friends then anyway—there was always work to do. Now, however, I had time to have a friend. Even though Johannes did not talk about himself, I was beginning to know him. Sometimes I even returned his teasing.

"Before you can have a daughter, you must first find a wife," I replied, and then added with a twinkle in my eyes, "But what girl would have you?"

Johannes pretended to be crushed by my words. He buried his face in his hands, then suddenly looked up.

"My ma always told me I was the most handsome of boys. Finding a wife should be no problem for one so good looking," he said.

Johannes leaned back, crossed his arms, and smiled smugly.

Papa sat watching us, enjoying our banter. I looked at him for help. What should I say next? Papa just grinned.

I turned back to Johannes. He was definitely handsome with his dark brown eyes and hair. Silently I agreed with his ma, but I dared not say that. Instead I said, "Tell me about your mama. What is she doing now?"

His eyes became distant, sad.

"Ma and my little sister, Katrina, are dead. Two years ago, when I was twelve, they died during the winter. They were not strong enough to survive the cold and starvation."

"Oh," I mumbled, sorry I'd asked.

But Johannes seemed relieved to talk and continued, "The Communist leaders do not care about us peasants. They only want to use us for their own profit."

His words were bitter.

"Ja, that is one reason we are leaving," I said, understanding his feelings.

"And that is one reason we are helping you. After a year of sitting and crying, Pa and I decided to get busy. We want to help people escape Russia so we joined the group which runs this secret escape route. Perhaps we will prevent death or prison from separating other families."

I looked at the stubborn set of his jaw and the determined look in his eyes. I liked him even better than before.

"Thank-you!" I said, softly.

"There are many like us," he explained. "Some

drive oxen, some deliver messages, some provide shelters. Are you ready for a night off this creaky, old cart? We should be nearing a shelter."

Suddenly his face became tense, straining to hear.

"Listen!" he said, urgently.

I held my breath. There was a distant, rushing noise. Quickly it grew louder. I glanced at Papa. His eyes were wide with dread, looking ahead of us.

Then I saw it, too—a wall of rain rushing toward us.

Chapter 13

We were drenched in seconds. Our clothes were filled with water, stiff and heavy. It was too late to look for shelter. We sat shivering, hopelessly wondering when the rain would stop.

Suddenly a face appeared beside me, peering into the wagon.

"People, you must get off this cart! Move—at once!"

The voice was strong, demanding. It shook us from the miserable, wet trance. I jumped to my knees and squinted through the rain running down my face.

A man in a uniform stood straight and tall beside the wagon. A soldier. Dread swept over me.

"Off now!" he commanded again, sounding impatient. "Hurry, we must not be seen."

Like the oxen blindly following their leader, the cart passengers obeyed. Silently, one by one, they climbed over the side of the cart and slipped to the soggy ground.

I watched Papa get off, grab his violin, and then help the little ones and Taty, but when my turn came, I froze. Johannes quickly pulled me to my feet and held my arm as I swung one leg over the edge.

"You must obey for your own good. Do not worry,"

he whispered. "Just go along with Commandant Froehl."

My eyes snapped angrily! After all we'd gone through to get this far, how could I cooperate with a Red soldier? What if he would send us back to Chukov . . . or worse? No, I was ready to fight first.

Johannes saw the anger in my eyes, and his grip tightened on my arm. "Please, Lisenka, go now quietly. I will explain later," he whispered.

I turned away. Papa caught my hand as I swung my other leg over the cart's edge. He kept hold of it until I looked at him. Then Papa flashed me his "practicing patience" smile. I sighed and obediently slipped down and followed through the mud behind him and the others. Johannes stayed back to help his pa with the oxen.

After a few minutes' walk, the silhouette of a barn loomed above us. I fought down hope. The barn will not be a shelter for us. No, I said to myself, soldiers push us around. They do not give us shelter . . . unless to do us harm.

The soldier, Commandant Froehl, spoke, "Here we are! Hurry in people. It is warm and dry. I have supper almost ready!"

This must be a trick, I thought. Why would he want to help us?

But I did not waste time doubting. Like the rest of the peasants, I hurried into the barn, relieved to escape the pelting rain. I stopped just inside the door, keeping an eye on the exit.

I rubbed the water from my eyes and blinked

quickly. Was I seeing clearly? The rest had stopped to stare, too.

A stove, glowing warmly, was set in the middle of the floor. From it floated the aroma of hot, vegetable stew.

"Come in! Come in!" urged Commandant Froehl, his voice now inviting. "Warm yourselves by the stove. Dry your wet clothes. I have blankets to wrap yourselves in."

Papa and Taty hurried nearer the stove and began to pull the dripping clothes off Yurgi and Alya. Whether this was a trap or not, they needed to warm the little ones. Their lips were turning blue. The other peasants also busily peeled off their wet, outer clothes. Commandant Froehl hustled around offering help and blankets.

Numbly I watched. Tears filled my eyes. I remembered our warm stove at home and the hot suppers Taty cooked for us there. Why did we leave, I thought sadly. Wet and shivering, I was miserable and suddenly wanted to be home—home where we could be dry and sleep on our own straw mattresses. At home I had been alone with Papa, Taty, and the little ones, not herded like animals with a bunch of peasants. My shoulders began to heave with silent, deep sobs.

A gentle hand reached out and patted my shoulder. I turned to find Johannes, his eyes wide with concern, standing beside me. Forgetting my shyness, I threw myself against him and burst into tears.

Johannes awkwardly stroked my hair until my crying calmed. Embarrassed, I stepped back. What must he think of me? I didn't know what to say.

Johannes broke the strained silence. "Lisenka, are you feeling better now?"

"Ja," I answered, keeping my eyes on the floor.

"This barn is safe," Johannes replied. "You can relax. Commandant Froehl is on our side. He's part of our secret team and was told by a messenger to expect us."

I gasped. A soldier, dressed like Chukov, could not be on our side. "Are you sure?" I asked. "How do you know we can trust him?"

"He has sheltered many of our passengers in the past. Ja, we can trust him. He is a Russian soldier, but he is not a Communist. He secretly risks his life to help people like you escape the terrors of Communism."

Relief flooded over me. Johannes smiled warmly, but his teeth were chattering. My teeth were chattering too. Suddenly we both burst into giggles.

"Why are we standing here, shivering, when a warm fire awaits us?" Johannes asked.

He grabbed my hand and pulled me toward the stove. Warmth surrounded me.

Chapter 14

The next morning the sky was clear. Even before there was a hint of the sun's rays showing in the east, Papa, Gerhardt, and the other men switched the wet straw on the cart for dry straw from the barn. Johannes was hitching the oxen. I stood watching the activity, content with my life once more. Our stomachs were filled with warm biscuits and coffee from Commandant Froehl's stove. We had loaves of bread in our knapsacks again, and we were rested. Ja, life was good.

"Hop up!" Papa said, grinning and boosting me into the cart. "The Lord has been very good to us, huh, Lisenka?"

"Ja, Papa," I said. "He sends the rain and the sunshine . . . and Commandant Froehl!"

Papa chuckled and then, patting my hand, turned to help the others. The women and children had gathered to board the cart, too. I noticed that Johannes had stopped to listen to Papa and me, then turned to finish the hitching.

Once everyone was on the cart, Papa stood quietly talking with Commandant Froehl. They stood away from us, speaking softly, so I could not hear. Papa's eyes were serious, and his face lined with concern.

Then he smiled, shook Commandant Froehl's hand and said, aloud, "Thank-you for your concern, Commandant. You are serving the Lord by helping your fellow Russians. May God continue to protect you."

Papa jumped on, Gerhardt called from in front of the oxen, "Are we ready?" And Johannes swung himself over the side of the cart and planted himself beside me.

As we began to roll away from the barn, Commandant Froehl stood in the shadows of the doorway waving.

We settled in for another long ride. I couldn't remember how many days we'd traveled before this, and I had no idea how many lay ahead, but I did know once more that God traveled with us.

I glanced at Papa's face; it no longer looked troubled.

Then I looked at Johannes. He was deep in thought and frowning.

"Why so glum?" I asked. The day seemed full of promise to me.

He sighed sadly, then said, "How can you believe in God, Lisenka, after all you've suffered?"

His serious tone surprised me, but his question was even more disturbing. Before I could answer, he continued, "I once believed in God's goodness, but when Ma and Katrina died, God no longer seemed good. After awhile God no longer seemed real. I cannot believe in him now."

I studied Johannes. He was again a stranger to me.

The teasing, smiling face that I had grown to love was replaced with a face filled with despair. What sadness his smiles had been hiding, I thought, and I searched my soul for words to cheer him. But I was at a loss for words. This time Johannes did not have words to fill the silence either. He turned away when he saw my confusion. Gloom settled over us, and we rode on, lost in our own thoughts.

Hours passed. Gerhardt and Johannes switched places once and then switched again. The rest of us did not get to stretch, and my spine was beginning to press through my skin. I felt a desperate need to move, turning one way and then the other.

"We will be stopping soon, Lisenka," Johannes said, noticing my squirming. "With the roads so muddy Pa felt we had to skip our morning break to make up for the slow pace."

I looked ahead of the oxen and saw the soupy mud that was once a road. "I guess I should be thankful to be riding in comfort," I said, "and not plodding through the mud."

Johannes stuck one of his legs into the air. It was covered with mud almost to his hips. "That's for sure!" he said, smiling for the first time since morning.

"Haa!" Gerhardt yelled sharply to the oxen. The oxen swerved left, but it was too late. The cart's right wheels sank into a deep mud bed that Gerhardt had only spied at the last minute. The hitch groaned as the oxen struggled to keep moving. With a creak and a lurch, the cart stopped dead.

Without hesitating Johannes swung over the cart's side. He sank in the mud past his knees. "I will push, Pa," he said.

"Let us help, too," Papa said, scrambling stiffly to his feet.

"No, no, folks. No need for all of us to take a mud bath," Gerhardt said with a chuckle. "We will give the oxen a minute to regain their strength, and then, with a little shove from my son, off we'll go!"

I was relieved that the cart stood still. I rolled over on my hands and knees and stretched my back up like a cat. It felt wonderful.

"Ready, folks?" Gerhardt called shortly, and I braced myself on the edge of the cart, still on my knees.

"Get up!" he called and the oxen strained forward.

Johannes was straining, too, lifting and pushing the cart from behind the rear wheel. The veins on his neck stuck out with the effort, and sweat beads popped out on his face, but we were beginning to move.

To keep a firm grip, Johannes stepped forward, but at the same moment one of the oxen lost its footing in the slimy mud. The cart sank backwards.

Johannes' face froze in pain, and with an agonizing scream he bent over. For an instant I did not understand; then I screamed, "His foot! The cart has rolled onto Johannes' foot! Please, somebody help him!"

Chapter 15

The afternoon sun touched the brown landscape with pink tones. The cart passengers looked pink, too, except for Johannes. The sun could not disguise his pale, strained face. I kept a careful watch, gently bracing him when the cart rocked, holding his hand when he groaned in pain. I could not help shuddering; his pain hurt me, too.

After the cart's wheel had smashed Johannes' foot, Papa and Gerhardt had wrapped it with rags, carefully packing straw around his foot to keep it cushioned and still. Gerhardt had given Johannes a little vodka to help ease his pain. It helped him sleep, but his face was still twisted in pain.

"Papa, can't we do something else?" I asked.

"This is the best we can do now, little one, but we will soon cross the border into Poland," Papa said, then hesitated. A flicker of concern crossed his face.

"There in the big city of Lyublin, perhaps, a doctor can help Johannes," Papa continued.

Papa's words did not encourage me. I heard the doubt in his voice, and tears pushed to the corners of my eyes. What if Johannes never walks again? How will he get along with only one foot? The tears escaped and ran down my face.

"He sleeps, Lisenka," Taty said in her soft voice. "Already his body is beginning to heal."

I looked again at Johannes' face. Did it look a little more relaxed? Maybe. I closed my eyes and silently prayed, "Please, God, heal Johannes' foot and bring him back to faith in you."

When I opened my eyes, I saw Papa fumbling with the cords tied around his violin. I watched puzzled. I glanced at the other passengers; their faces were somber. This did not seem like the right time for music.

"We have come too close to despair," Papa said, a smile brightening his face.

I noticed for the first time how deep the wrinkles on Papa's face had sunk and how more gray hairs speckled his dark brown locks. The journey had been rough on him, but once more he mustered the strength to cheer us.

"We have many reasons to be thankful, folks," Papa continued. "Johannes could have been hurt more seriously, but he was not. Soon he will see a doctor. Our long journey by ox cart is nearly over. We have been protected from arrest. No thieves have robbed us. We have found wonderful new friends."

Papa winked at me. I smiled.

"Friends," Papa said, "it is truly a time for singing."

All the while Papa was talking, he was tuning the violin. Now he began to play a sweet lullaby. It reminded me of the gentle flickering candlelight at home and of Papa's singing while Taty tucked me and the little ones into our straw mattresses.

Those long forgotten words again entered my mind as I began to hum the melody:

"From heav'n above to earth I come
To bear good news to every home.
Glad tidings of great joy I bring
Whereof I now will say and sing."

The heaviness was lifting from my heart. Papa's music was what I needed, and when he started verse two, I had to sing along softly.

"To you this night is born a child
Of Mary chosen virgin mild.
This little child of lowly birth
Shall be the joy of all the earth."

Taty, smiling, joined in the singing. The little ones, stared with surprise, but their faces were beaming. Several other passengers chimed in. We sang softly, carefully. Our voices must not carry too far.

"This is the Christ, our God and Lord,
Who in all need shall aid afford.
He will himself your Savior be
From all your sins to set you free."

Smiles filled the faces of the passengers now. Papa's music was medicine for our souls. I turned to Johannes. His eyes were open, looking at me.

"Martin Luther," he said.

"What?"

"Martin Luther wrote that song. My ma used to sing it to me. We were Lutheran until . . ." Johannes voice strained in pain as the cart rocked.

I was so surprised at his words that I forgot his pain. "We are Lutherans, too," I responded. "We are leaving Russia because Papa felt we could no longer worship God here."

"You have gone through all this just so you could worship God?" He looked at me, his mouth hanging open in shock. "Is it really that important?"

***

Chapter 16

My eyes opened slowly. What was wrong? Above me hung the familiar canopy of night; Johannes moaned softly beside me, and the straw of the oxen cart rustled under his slight movement.

Everything is still, I suddenly realized; we've stopped moving. Soft whispers floated from beyond the cart. When I peeked over the edge to see who was there, only shadows, swaying in the tall grass, were visible. Still I heard the whispers and strained to see through the dark.

Two shadows began to take shape and move toward me. I caught my breath in fear, then recognized Papa's form and beside him, Gerhardt. They stopped next to the cart, almost beside me.

"You saw where the fence is. We must not cut the wires or even give any evidence that anybody has gone through it," Gerhardt said softly. "If the border guards suspect that people are fleeing Russia through this deserted farmland, yet another escape route will be blocked."

We're at the border already, I thought, amazed. Papa had said soon, but not tonight.

"I want you, Pavel, to help the cart passengers over the fence, covering your tracks as best you can," Gerhardt continued. "Then lead the group to the right a couple hundred rods. Wait under the large oak tree for Johannes and me. You will be able to see it."

"And what of you and Johannes? How will you get past the guards on the main road? Commandant Froehl cautioned us that the border is tightening, that they've increased the number of guards and the regulations. They seem to be intent on stopping any more of us from escaping," Papa said.

"We have the papers which should get the two of us through. The papers say we're going to Lyublin to get supplies, but they don't say we can't take a bit of company along," he added, chuckling.

Papa smiled, too, then saw me peeking over the edge. "So little lady, you're in on the plans once more, are you?" he said, reaching over and tugging on a braid. "Well, it's time to move. You might as well be the first off the cart."

When I stood to swing off the cart, Johannes came instantly awake and grabbed my legs, holding me tightly. He began to sob loudly. "No, she can't leave me. Please, don't take her away from me."

His voice rushed through the still night air, sending a shiver of fear through me and startling the others awake. Quickly I sat down beside Johannes to quiet him.

"Hush, Johannes, wake up. You're putting us all in danger," I said, softly, urgently.

I sat brushing his hair back from his damp forehead, and slowly he relaxed.

Turning to Papa, I said, "Take the others first, I will follow later."

"No," Johannes screamed again. "Do not leave me."

This time I could not calm him. Realizing that keeping Johannes quiet was our only chance, I said, "Papa, I will stay with the cart."

Papa stared at me, his face a mixture of concern and pride.

"We will get through, Papa," I said, drawing on strength above my own. "Remember—with God all things are possible."

***

The cart was empty except for Johannes and me; its rattles and creaking seemed to grow louder as Gerhardt led the oxen the last two miles to the border.

When the lantern lights of the guards came into view, I pulled my shawl over my face and faked sleep as Gerhardt had told me. Johannes held my hand tightly, but he was breathing calmly. I hoped he was asleep.

After the cart came to rest, I could hear Gerhardt rustling papers and then talking with the guards.

"I am taking my son along to Lyublin so that a doctor there can attend to his foot. He had an accident a few days ago," Gerhardt stated, matter-of-factly.

Through my closed eye lids, I could see the light from the lanterns growing brighter and swinging back and forth above us so that the guards could check the cart's contents.

"Why are there two children here?" inquired a strangely familiar voice.

"My son is very ill and begged to have his little sister along to care for him," Gerhardt answered, sadly. "I could not deny him that."

Unexpectedly, Johannes moaned and turned his fever blotched face toward the lantern.

"What harm can a little girl do?" asked one soldier.

"Ja, I guess you are right," responded the other, reluctantly.

That voice, I thought. I could never forget that voice. It was Chukov. A lump of panic twisted in my throat. I caught my breath. I could feel Chukov's beady eyes boring down on me. Is my face completely covered with my shawl, I wondered, as prickles of fear crawled across my scalp? I prayed it was and did not stir further.

It seemed forever before someone spoke again. It was the hateful voice of Chukov. "Have you by chance seen a family from Prebnow during your travels?" Chukov asked Gerhardt, suddenly acting friendly. "They escaped my village, and I have been sent to intercept them. The man, named Pavel, is extremely dangerous to the good of Russia and must be punished."

There was silence from Gerhardt.

No, don't believe that liar, I silently begged of Gerhardt.

Then came Gerhardt's deliberate answer, "A dangerous family? No, I can't say that I've seen anyone like that."

Chapter 17

Johannes' fever of the night cooled as daylight flooded over us. He did not remember screaming or demanding that I stay with him. It seemed funny now, and we giggled as the oxen cart carried us into Poland, away from the grasps of terror and Chukov.

Papa went pale when Gerhardt told him of our close brush with Chukov and then hugged me tight. "I guess God was giving you a chance to say 'Goodbye.' Why did you sleep through it?" Papa teased.

During the next few days on the oxen76 cart, I found I had much to say to Johannes. He wanted to know every detail about our decision to leave Russia. He needed to hear how we saw God's hand in the closing of our school, in my eating of the whole sausage, and in Chukov's taking our Bible.

While he rested with his foot propped high to relieve the pain, I told him about the little green pumpkins, about the Schmidts, about Chukov's attempt to stop our escape from the village, and about God's way of stopping him. Then I also told him about God's greatest work of rescue—how he sent Jesus to be our Savior.

I did much more of the talking than I ever had before. Johannes listened intently, but he did not share any of his thoughts.

Soon we rumbled into Lyublin, where we could safely take a train. There my eyes stared in wonder at the big buildings and the crowds of people. It was bewildering. I'd never seen anything like it! The sights made me forget that good-byes were very near.

As we approached the train station, Johannes reached for my hand. His grasp was strong, but his smile was shaky. Was it pain from his foot or from the final good-bye? My smile was also shaky. I knew why. I did not want to say good-bye to my dear friend.

Johannes spoke. "Lisenka, you have brightened our journey, and you have given me much to think about. You are a wonderful friend."

I nodded, unable to speak.

"Do not worry about me or my foot. If God can work out so much for your good, I'm sure he'll take care of your blundering friend," he said with a sparkle that I hadn't seen since the accident.

I nodded again, and Johannes began to laugh.

"Lisenka, you have not been at a loss for words for several days. Did I listen all the words out of you?"

The cart came to a stop.

"Everybody out," Gerhardt said cheerfully. The cart buzzed with excitement as the passengers quickly gathered their few belongings and began to scramble over the side of the cart. It was the day we had been waiting for. A day to rejoice.

My joy was wrapped in sadness. My sadness was wrapped in joy. Finally I could speak. "I am afraid to leave you. We do not know what the future will bring for us, but I will not forget you. I will always thank the Lord for your friendship and pray that he keeps you safe—forever."

Papa shook Gerhardt's hand and then reached into the cart to pat Johannes' shoulder. "You're a fine boy, Johannes, and I know the Lord will bring you through this hard time."

Johannes blinked quickly and squeezed my hand more tightly. As tears blurred my eyes, I gently pulled away from his grasp and climbed over the cart's edge.

"Time to get this boy to a doctor," Gerhardt said. "Haa!" The oxen began to slowly pull them away . . . and out of our lives.

Johannes waved, and so did I. Then from the cart floated a melody. The words were clear:

"This is the Christ our God and Lord,
Who in all need shall aid afford;
He will himself your Savior be
From all your sins to set you free."

Papa stopped short and stared after the cart. Then he looked at me proudly. "The Lord has used you to touch that young man's heart, Lisenka. What miracles he can work through us frail people!"

"I did nothing, Papa, just told Johannes about how God worked in our lives."

"That's all we can do," Papa said. "God only asks us to share his Good News. He's the one who touches the hearts."

Chapter 18

A deafening whistle split the air and the floor shook as a black monster roared passed. Smoke billowed from its stack, and steam hissed from behind its giant wheels. The wheels screeched to a stop beside us. I looked at them. They were taller than Papa! Then I scanned the black, seething train. It was bigger than I ever imagined. A sharp gasp caught in my throat.

The little ones and I stood clinging to each other in a shivering huddle. Our bundles, everything we owned, were piled at our feet on the station platform.

"Save me, Senka," Yurgi screamed and wrapped his little arms around my waist tighter. Alya also pushed in closer. Fear gripped me, too, but I kept it hidden from the little ones.

"It's just a train," I said, straining to speak above the noise. "Remember, Papa told us all about them. This train will carry us to a big ship. The big ship will take us to America."

"America," I said again, more softly. After the tedious weeks of being packed into the oxen cart, I'd almost forgotten about America. An excited shiver ran through me—we are going to America!

Alya looked at me with surprise. "America!" She asked, "Are we really getting close to America?"

"One step closer," I said with a smile, remembering Papa's words from so long ago as we started our journey. "We are one step closer."

The train waited quietly now, and Alya and Yurgi eased their hold, but they did not let go.

"When will Papa and Mama come back?" Yurgi asked. "I'm hungry!"

I could see Taty's white kerchief at a fruit stand down the street. Papa was not in sight, but I knew he was buying our train tickets. I glanced timidly at the giant train and shuddered. Where will I ever get the courage to climb inside that fiery monster?

Just then Papa, waving five tickets high in the air, hurried around the corner of the station.

"What luxuries await us!" he said. "Just think, children. We will each have our own seat with lots of room to stretch our legs. A roof will protect us from the rain, and there will even be a stove to keep us warm."

I looked from Papa's excited face to the vibrating black monster. Steam suddenly gushed from underneath it. I jumped back, startled. Papa reached out and took my cold hand, "It will be safe, Lisenka." he said softly.

"No, Papa," I couldn't help saying, "I think I'd rather go on by oxen cart. I don't think I'm going to enjoy 'luxuries.'"

Papa's eyes twinkled, but he did not laugh. Wisely, he changed the subject. "See this money?" he said, holding up his coin pouch. "This money which is buying our trip to America has been hidden for years. It's the money I earned to bring you and your mama to America. Oh! This is a wonderful day! At last the money is being used for its rightful purpose."

Papa stood there, glowing with happiness; then he saw Taty crossing the street, and he scampered over to help her.

Just like a boy. Papa is acting just like a boy, I thought. I swallowed my fear and said to the little ones, "See how happy Papa is? This is a wonderful day. Riding on the train will be fun. Right?"

They nodded obediently. I almost convinced myself.

Before Taty could show us what she'd bought, a man wearing a red hat stepped onto the platform and blew a shrill whistle.

"There's our signal," Papa said, gathering up our bundles and handing them out to us. "Time to get on board."

My stomach felt as if it hit bottom and then leaped into my throat. My knees turned to jelly, but as Papa put his arm around my shoulders and pulled me toward the train, my legs obeyed.

Up the dark, little steps they carried me and into a long narrow room. There were wooden benches on both sides and an aisle up the middle. At the far end a porter in a brown suit was making a fire in the stove.

It's just the way Papa said, I thought, and sighed with relief. I sat next to the window, and in a moment the train jerked and then began to roll away from the station. As I munched a juicy, red apple, Lyublin disappeared behind us, and small farms flashed past my eyes. The world was moving past me at an unbelievable speed!

"Now we are crossing the farmlands of Poland," Papa explained. "Tomorrow we will be in Germany, very near Martin Luther's homeland. Next we will cross Luxemburg, and then we'll be entering France. At LeHavre, France, we'll board our ship."

My mind could not understand the big changes that were happening. The names Papa tossed out so casually meant very little to me.

But then Papa continued, "In three days we'll cover as many miles as we traveled in a month by oxen cart. Do you still wish for the 'luxuries' of the oxen cart, Lisenka?"

I giggled as I remembered my silly fear. "No, Papa," I said. "The train is a much better way to travel. Will the ship be even nicer?"

Chapter 19

I looked again at the unfamiliar words on the sign. I wondered if some day I would be able to read this.

"This is in French," Papa said and scratched his head, studying the words for a minute. Then he pointed to one of the words. "Paris, that's the name of our ship. And here," he pointed again, "is today's date, 1927 December 9. Paris sails today for America."

He looked at Taty, a grin filling his face, and added, "And we will be on board." Then he squeezed my hand more tightly.

We were a timid little group, smiling broadly at each other, as we stood on the wooden planks of the dock in LeHavre, France. In front of us loomed Paris, our ship to America.

"I have never seen such a ship," Papa exclaimed. "The ticket agent said that Paris is almost 800 feet long. Magnificent!"

I looked at Papa with surprise. He'd been using such new words lately. But magnificent was probably a fitting word for Paris. Even though the ship was so huge that it could have swallowed our big, black train, I felt no fear now. Paris rocked gently like a duck floating on a smooth pond. The freshly painted sides glistened almost as much as the water rippling beyond. With its streamers of flags snapping in the breeze on the top deck and its lines of eager travelers already filing up the gangplanks, the ship looked like a mansion of heaven with people lining up to get into it.

"May we board, too?" I asked Papa, anxious to join the excitement.

"Ja, little lady."

I skipped ahead of them and hurried back— skipped ahead again and hurried back again. Why did they move so slowly? I reached the plank first and tipped my head back, looking up—way up. The ship towered above us now, higher than the highest tree, almost touching the clouds.

"Oh," I gasped, as the rest caught up. "Must we go so high?"

"From the top deck, Lisenka, you will be able to see many miles. It will be magnificent. You'll see," Papa answered and took the lead up the gangplank. Taty and the little ones followed.

I glanced once more at the towering ship. Papa knows what he's doing, I said to myself. This will be magnificent. With that thought, I bounded up the gangplank, too.

But the confusion on deck was overwhelming. People were rushing here and there. Sailors were yelling at each other in a strange language. Supplies were being swung on board. I grabbed the tail of Papa's coat in panic. This jumble of people and activities was no place to get separated from Papa.

He gave my shoulder a pat, asked directions of a man in uniform and then headed toward a double door with me for a tail. Taty also stuck close, dragging the two little ones along. They, like me, were busy looking everywhere at once.

As the doors swung shut behind us, Papa stopped in amazement. "This ship is more magnificent than I can believe," he exclaimed. "Just look at this."

We crowded around Papa to get a better view. Soft light reflected off various shades of wood paneling on the walls of the huge room, and across the room mirrors reflected the wood. But in front of us was the real wonder. A wide stairway with fancy, ironwork railings descended gracefully into a huge room.

In Russia we had had one or two steps to get into a house. During our journey there had been four narrow steps into our train car, and in LeHavre, our small hotel had had long, dark stairs leading to the second floor. But this was baffling.

"Papa, why do we need such a grand stairway?" I asked.

"It is simply for beauty," he answered. "People traveling first and second class will be able to relax here. I just wanted you all to see how grand Paris is, before we go into our third class state room. That is the area for us emigrants."

Papa led the way again through a maze of halls. Ours was a large room filled with narrow benches, one stacked above another. There were other emigrants already buzzing about.

"These are bunk beds," Papa explained, pointing

to the stacked benches. "Do you want a top or a bottom bunk, Lisenka?"

"Oh, top, please," I said quickly. Papa led me to an empty one. How exciting it would be to sleep so far off the floor.

While Papa and Taty claimed four more—Papa on a top and the rest in bottom bunks, I scrambled up a little ladder to mine.

Sprawling on my back, I studied the pipes and wires that ran overhead. Where did they come from? Where did they go? They were a puzzle to me. Then I stretched as far as I could. My bunk was so long that my feet and hands did not touch the ends. I closed my eyes and rubbed the soft, cloth pad under me. Third class is not magnificent, but this is luxury, I thought, remembering another of Papa's new words.

A loud horn sounded, and then the ship began to shake.

"Come on," Papa called. "The engines have started. Let's go on deck to say good-bye to the old country."

I jumped down and grabbed the little ones' hands. Papa linked arms with Taty, and together we climbed the narrow steps to the deck.

A blast of cool, salt air hit my face. Overhead white birds were swooping and diving. I ran to the rail, took a deep breath, and then looked down. Magnificent! Far below, little waves bounced off the side of the ship. Two smaller boats were pulling Paris away from the dock.

"As soon as we're in deeper water, Paris will be able to use her big propellers. Then see how fast we move," Papa said.

Soon we began moving more quickly. I looked over the side again and saw the little boats turning back toward shore. Two white streaks in the shape of a V flowed in the water behind us.

"See that V in the water?" Papa asked. "That's our V . . . our V for victory. We have escaped the old country. God has given us the victory."

We stood there watching the buildings of LeHavre get smaller and smaller. I glanced at Taty. Tears were quietly rolling down her cheek. Papa noticed, too.

"Why are you crying, Taty?" he asked tenderly, pulling her close. "We are victorious."

"Ja, we have won a few battles," she replied, "but how many battles still face us? Will I be strong enough to keep fighting?"

"I will help you, Taty. I will help you be strong," I said with confidence and flung my arms around them both.

Chapter 20

Papa's voice was far away. "Lisenka," he said, stroking my damp forehead, "try to be strong."

I could sense Papa was kneeling beside me on the floor where I'd collapsed that first day. When seasickness struck me, the top bunk was too far off the floor for me. My rolling stomach had wanted no part of a swaying bunkbed.

Be strong. Be strong, I said to myself. I tried, but I could not move. Finally, I forced my heavy eyelids open.

"Hello, little one," Papa said warmly and took my hands in his. "Come, Lisenka; let's go up on the deck for some fresh air. You'll feel better."

As he began to pull me up from the floor, a new wave of nausea swept over me. Quickly, I grabbed the bucket. Dry heaves shook my body, but after six days of being sick, my stomach had nothing left to push out. I heaved again and again, then fell weakly back onto the floor.

Papa sat beside me, stroking one of my hands. His eyes were tired and far away. I knew he was thinking about our voyage. A few hours after we left LeHavre, Taty got sick . . . then me and the little ones. Papa remained well and took care of all of us, comforting us, emptying our buckets, patiently forcing us to drink water, a few drops at a time.

"Papa," I whispered, "how are Taty and the little ones?"

"They are very weak," Papa said, "especially Taty." Deep concern creased his face when he looked at Taty. "But they are sleeping peacefully now." Papa added, trying to sound hopeful.

"I let Taty down," I said. "I promised to help her be strong, and I'm too weak to even help myself." I sniffled and quickly brushed a tear from my cheek. Papa must not see my tears. At least I could be strong enough not to cry.

"Lisenka, we are all only weak people. We can promise strength, but only God is capable of giving it. Will you join me in prayer?"

I closed my eyes and listened carefully to Papa's words, "Lord, we know you are the one who fights our battles, and you are the one who gives us the victory. Taty and the little ones are losing their battles, Lord. We need your help now. They have not eaten for days. Before much longer . . ." Papa's voice broke into a sob. Then he continued, "Please, Lord, please help them to escape this sickness before it is too late."

Papa cried. I could not bear to see him this sad, and I turned toward the bunk. Exhausted, I fell asleep once more—this time into a deep, quiet sleep.

Later, when I awoke, I heard soft talking. It was Papa.

"Tomorrow we will be entering New York's harbor.

There at Ellis Island we will be examined by doctors to see if we are healthy enough to be allowed into America."

"And what will happen if one of us is not?" It was Taty's voice, weak and fearful.

"Then that person will get a chalk mark on his back and be held on Ellis Island until he can be shipped back to his old country."

Silence followed.

"That is why you must eat, Taty. I thank the Lord that your seasickness is passing, but your strength is gone. Please, come with me to the dining room."

Suddenly, I was hungry, too. "Papa, may I come along, too?"

"Me, too!" said Alya from her bunk.

"Senka, take me, too!" Yurgi said.

Papa twirled to look at all of us and then said, "Finally, your bodies have gotten used to the roll of the ocean. Do you think you'll be stricken with land sickness tomorrow in America?" He chuckled, seeming once more like my papa.

Our legs were not strong enough to carry us so Papa first helped Taty and Yurgi into the dining room and then returned for Alya and me. The room was filled with long wooden tables. We sat on a bench at one of them.

As a platter of food was placed in front of us, Papa exclaimed, "Well, look at this! We're having a real German feast: pork hocks, potatoes, sauerkraut. Eat slowly. Give your stomachs time to handle food again."

First I sampled a little bit of potato. It was wonderful. I took some sauerkraut with my next bite. It tasted so good that I had to force myself to eat slowly. Bite by bite I could feel my strength growing. I glanced at Taty. A slight smile touched her pale lips.

"Pavel," she said, turning to Papa, "remember when we were children? We often had such feasts. I am happy our children will get to have feasts, too, in America."

Papa nodded and smiled. Was it a sad smile?

Taty's hand shook as she slowly took a bite. Her skin was chalky white on her thin face.

Will we even get into America? Please, Lord, let us get into America.

After supper the sun was setting. We strolled slowly on the deck. We walked together, holding onto each other for support. When we stopped by the edge, I leaned against the rail, looking toward the back of the ship.

Ja, I said to myself, the V is still following us.

Papa must have read my thoughts. "God's victory is still with us, huh, Lisenka? He is giving you new strength, too. What do you think? Will you be strong enough to try that top bunk tonight?"

Chapter 21

"Wake up!" Papa cried urgently.

I sat up in my top bunk and rubbed my eyes. "What is it, Papa?" I mumbled, but he had already moved on to Alya and Yurgi, shaking them awake, too, with the same urgent voice.

By now I was wide awake. What could be the matter? Quickly I looked at Taty's bunk. She was getting up. The little ones were tumbling out of their bunks, too.

"Papa, what is the matter?" I asked again, more loudly.

"The matter?" Papa asked. He pranced back to me and swung me down, giving me an extra twirl before he set me on the floor. "Nothing is the matter. Quick, come on deck. We're here. The Lady is greeting us! It's America!"

His excitement flooded over us. Together we tumbled up the narrow stairs. The deck was packed with a mass of people, chattering, laughing, crying. Papa slowly threaded his way through the crowd. We made sure to stick close. At the side of the ship, Papa lifted Yurgi to his shoulders while Alya and I peeked between the people who were standing at the railing.

To the left was a huge copper statue, tinted slightly green. It was the Statue of Liberty. Papa had told me all about this wonderful lady. She stood gracefully on the small island where she'd been set many years ago. She had greeted many immigrants in the past. Today she was welcoming us to America. We are in America!

"Is it God?" Yurgi asked. His eyes were big with excitement.

Papa looked at Taty with a smile, put his arm around her, and pulled her tight. "No, Yurgi," Papa said gently. "She is not God, but she does give me hope. I know that in America I will have the freedom to worship God!"

"Freedom," I whispered. Suddenly words popped into my head. Papa had said they were printed on the Lady's base. "Give me your tired, your poor, your huddled masses yearning to breathe free!"

I breathed deeply. The air was fresh. It smelled like . . . freedom.

Our ship passed another small island set low in the water. There were many buildings on the island, but one red, brick building held my attention. It was lovely with four towers. Was it a mansion?

As I stared, Papa pointed to the island and said, "That is Ellis Island. We will be ferried back there for our examinations. That is our door to America."

"I have heard that it is also called 'Heartbreak Island,'" Taty whispered. Then she lowered her voice still more, but I strained to hear.

"Pavel," she said, "promise me this. If I do not pass the examinations, please take the children into America. I will return to my friends in Russia. I will be fine with my old friends, but, please, give the children a chance to have freedom."

I could not hear Papa's reply. The mansion blurred as tears filled my eyes. No, it won't happen. God will give us victory. I fought down the fear which crept through my mind. Make me strong, I prayed, and the fear faded.

I looked ahead and gasped. Giant buildings towered above the pier ahead. I picked out the tallest building and began to count the windows going up. "One . . . two . . . three . . . four . . . " I counted all the way to fourteen. "Papa," I exclaimed. "There are fourteen floors in that tall building. Fourteen! How can it be so tall?"

Papa smiled. "That's America. It's a land of wonder. People can do anything in America."

Before I had time to think about Papa's words, shouts filled the air. Officers on the ship were pushing the crowds of people into different groups. They yelled in many languages I did not understand, but then I heard familiar words, German words, "Move quickly! Hurry!"

"What is happening, Papa?"

"We must return to our room to gather our belongings and then wait for our turn to get off the ship. First and second class passengers are first."

I saw nicely dressed men and ladies lining up near exit gates. We climbed back down the narrow stairs with the other third class immigrants. As we sat on our bunks, waiting, a ship officer came through and pinned a numbered tag on each of us.

"That is to keep us all together at Ellis Island," Papa explained.

"Did those nicely dressed ladies and men have numbers, too?" I asked.

"No, little one," Papa answered, looking puzzled. "They do not need to go through Ellis Island."

Suddenly, I felt cheated—as if Papa had given the little ones hugs and had forgotten me. I wondered if America would hug the rich and forget about us poor peasants.

"Papa, are you sure that anyone, even the poor, can do anything in America?"

***

Chapter 22

"Move quickly! Hurry!" Again the ship echoed with the officers' commands. This time we were being herded with other poorly dressed immigrants onto a ferry. We were on our way to Ellis Island, our door to America—or will it be 'Heartbreak Island' for us, I wondered. The thrill we first felt this morning was gone. A deep dread had settled over us.

I dreaded the examinations that we'd soon face. I dreaded the thought that Taty might not pass. I dreaded an empty life in America—without Taty.

I stood at the rail and glanced behind me at the others sitting on the bench. Papa was holding both of Taty's hands. Their heads were bowed, probably in prayer. Quickly I, too, bowed my head. "Please, Lord, we have come so far and suffered so much that we just cannot be refused now. Please let us enter America. Let us all enter."

Approaching Ellis Island reminded me of things Papa had told me about Judgment Day. Ja, today is much like that, I realized. We can only trust God's grace to get us in.

Those thoughts helped me once more to push down my fear, but as our ferry pulled up to the dock, I could not slow my racing heart. The big, red brick building with the four towers stood in front of me. It was beautiful! Ja, I said to myself, even this close it does look like a mansion of heaven!

Again orders were shouted at us in many languages. I no longer listened to the jumbled words, just grabbed Yurgi's hand and followed Papa, Taty, and Alya. Papa and Taty had linked arms. They seemed so confident as they joined the mass of people filing off the ferry. I was glad to be the child, just following.

We passed under a long canopy and through the doors of the big building. A gigantic room loomed before us. It rang with strange words, crying, and screaming. Yurgi began to whimper so I lifted him to my hip and gently rubbed his back, but my eyes never stopped darting about, trying to see everything.

On the opposite wall hung a big red and white striped flag. It had a blue patch with white stars.

"That is our flag," Papa said proudly, "the stars and stripes of freedom." He stopped a moment just to look. The flag was so big that it could have draped over our whole house back in Russia.

"Magnificent," I whispered, and stood gawking until Taty nudged us ahead of her and Alya, keeping us safely packed between Papa and her.

Iron pipes divided the huge room into a maze of aisles. All around me people were shouting in languages I could not understand. A guard pointed Papa into one aisle, but when I tried to follow, the guard blocked my way. Papa did not notice and disappeared into his line. Panic rolled over me, and I could not see or hear or even think. The guard jabbered and pointed again. Taty pulled me in another direction to an aisle. It was filled with women and children.

"Slow down," a guard shouted at me in words I could finally understand. "Put down the child. He must walk."

I realized that this was the beginning of our examinations. Gently I put Yurgi on the floor. He walked timidly, clinging to my hand.

Ahead I saw two men, probably doctors, standing on each side of our rail dividers. They studied faces, hair, hands, and feet as the people, like animals going to a butchering, slowly filed past them. It scared me to look at those two men. Their stares were hard, studying every person closely, but not really seeing people. I tried to keep my eyes straight ahead and not look at them.

Just then one doctor took a piece of chalk and put an "L" on the right shoulder of a limping man. A few more people passed the doctor before he marked again with his chalk. This time it was an "X" on a little girl's right shoulder.

As I stared at that piece of chalk, it seemed to take on a power of its own. Every time the doctor used it, a ripple of fear passed from person to person back along the line until I quivered all the way down to my toes. I knew that chalk held the power to send us back to Russia. I also felt sure that if Taty could pass the chalk without a mark, we'd be through the door—the door into America.

As Taty approached the doctors, she stumbled. My breath caught in my throat. Don't collapse here, Taty, I silently pleaded. Immediately the doctors rushed to her. Taty steadied herself on the iron pipes and then nodded her thanks. She pointed to her long skirt, motioning that it had tripped her. I stared at her in amazement. Where in her weakness did she have this strength hidden? The doctors stepped back. The chalk disappeared into the big hand of one doctor as he swung his arm back to his side. Taty and Alya passed safely through.

I began to sigh in relief, but gulped instead. The hard stares of the men fastened on me, then on Yurgi. In my concern for Taty I'd forgotten that we too, must pass the chalk.

I pushed myself forward. Once more the chalk was raised—this time in front of my eyes.

Chapter 23

We trudged on through the line, passing another pair of doctors. Their stares did not scare me. The chalked "Sc" on Yurgi's right shoulder had numbed my fear.

Even as we approached the final doctor, the dreaded eye exam, I felt no fear. Alya screamed in pain when the doctor took her eyelids and folded them, one at a time, back over a hook-like tool. He looked deeply into each eye and then turned to Taty. Taty quietly endured her examination. Next it was Yurgi's turn. He screamed wildly and thrashed in my arms. A woman with dark hair and a kind face hurried over to help me hold him.

She smiled at me and said in my language, "This is the last test in your main examination. Here the doctor is checking for a dangerous eye disease. It will be over soon."

I nodded and stepped forward for my turn. The pain shot through my head—first from one eye, then the other. The kind woman had been right. It was over quickly.

The doctor said something to the woman, and she marked a piece of paper.

"You all passed the eye exam," she said and then

glanced sadly at Yurgi.

What does it matter, I thought, and looked once more at Yurgi's right shoulder. I didn't know what the "Sc" meant, but felt sure that the chalk mark had slammed shut our door to America.

Papa sat waiting on a wooden bench at the end of our aisle. When he saw us coming, he hurried over to Taty, turned her to see her right shoulder, and then with eyes raised toward heaven exclaimed, "Thank you, Lord!"

Finally, he looked at our grim faces and began to realize that all was not well.

"What is the matter?" he asked, frantically grabbing Taty's shoulders. Taty turned away and buried her face in Alya's hair, sobbing.

Then Papa looked at me. His straight-lipped smile told me he was struggling for patience. "What has happened, Lisenka?"

"It's Yurgi," I blurted out before I too burst into tears.

Papa knelt down and held his hands out to Yurgi. Yurgi bounded into his embrace. Papa glanced down at the "Sc" on Yurgi's shoulder and then hugged him tighter.

"This is not the end of our hope," Papa said, looking over Yurgi's head. "An 'Sc' means the doctors suspect Yurgi has a scalp disease, and they want to check him more carefully."

He released Yurgi. "Look here!" he said and pointed to two bald spots on Yurgi's head. "Remember when Yurgi tangled with that rooster? These bald spots are scars from that battle. I'm sure when the doctors see these closely, Yurgi, too, will pass!"

I smiled through my tears. Taty looked up, smiling, too. I remembered that day and suddenly couldn't hold back my giggles. "Remember how sweet Yurgi looked in Taty's kerchief?" I asked between giggles. Suddenly the whole family bursted into laughter. It felt good to laugh again, but people began to stare at us so Papa hushed us.

I pressed my hand to my mouth; giggles were still trying to bubble out.

"Herr Schallert?"

We turned to see the dark-haired, kind-faced woman, standing behind us. A smile was twitching on her lips. I wonder if she saw our silliness.

"My name is Elsa Bauer," she said. "Since I know German and English, I will help you talk to the doctors here. First we need to take your little boy to the specialist for further examinations. Would you or your wife want to accompany us?"

"I'll stay with the girls. You go with Yurgi," Papa said to Taty.

We watched as Elsa led them down a hall. Yurgi, who was not yet four, looked tiny walking between the two women. He held tightly to Taty's hand, but was smiling up at Elsa. I smiled as they disappeared around the corner. Yurgi was my baby, too. I'd played mother to him often since the time he was a little baby. I was happy Elsa was helping him now.

"Our first American friend," Papa said and settled back on the wooden bench to wait. We joined him. The wait was long.

"Will it be much longer?" Alya asked again.

"Soon," Papa answered.

It was the same question and answer I had heard several times already during our wait. Each time I became a little more worried. Good news could not take this long. I got up and paced toward the hall.

Two women were approaching. I recognized Taty's shawl and kerchief. Elsa was with her, but not Yurgi.

"Where is Yurgi?" I cried as I dashed toward them.

Taty's face was creased with worry.

"He will be kept a day or two in the hospital," Elsa explained. "He will get the best care and will be released soon. Don't worry. It will be fine."

Elsa's words made me feel better, but she could not hide the concern in her own eyes.

Elsa repeated her words to Papa when he hurried up to us.

"It is nothing. Can't the doctors see that?" Papa demanded.

"They suspect Yurgi has a contagious form of ringworm," Elsa said, "and want to watch those spots on his head. If, after a few days, the spots do not change, Yurgi will be released. Can you be patient a couple more days?"

"Patient?" Papa asked. "Oh, ja, we can be patient. We have had much practice at being patient."

He winked at me, trying to ease the tension. I didn't like his little joke.

"Papa, do some people have more patience than others?" I asked, "because I think my patience is all used up."

Chapter 24

The next morning I stared at the plateful of sausages, eggs, and biscuits set before me in the big dining room. Amazing! Here was the feast I'd promised myself so long ago when Gerhardt had teased me about breakfast. How far we'd traveled since that oxen cart.

Yesterday Elsa had led Papa, Taty, Alya, and me to our room. It had an electric light. We only had to pull the chain to flood the room with brightness. We also each had our own bed with smooth, white sheets, fluffy pillows, and as many blankets as we needed to keep warm. Before we even had time to explore the luxuries, Elsa had carried a big box into our room. Alya and I had danced in excitement as she unpacked the shoes, stockings, sweaters—more than I had ever seen.

"Oh, Elsa," I'd said as Alya and I danced around her, "This is too wonderful to believe. Thank you. Thank you."

She had sat back on her heels, her brown eyes sparkling. "You're welcome. You're welcome," she answered. "But these gifts are not from me. The Red Cross is providing them for you. I am just a volunteer, but I am very glad to be able to translate for you and to be your friend."

Elsa peered into the bottom of the box and said, "Just one more thing." She handed me a book. My hand began to shake as I took it.

Ja, it is true, I thought. I will learn to read here in America, but when I opened the book, I saw no familiar words.

Seeing my shocked look, Elsa had explained, "This book is written in English, the language you must learn here. Tomorrow I'll begin to teach you to read English."

***

And now it's "tomorrow," I thought. A broad smile spread across my face.

Suddenly a chuckle shook me from my thoughts. "You are getting much pleasure from your breakfast," Papa said, "Did you know it's even better when you stop staring at it and begin eating it?"

I smiled at Papa. He was funnier today.

"Ja," Taty said, not hearing the joke, "Soon Elsa will be here to take us to visit Yurgi. Eat up."

And I quickly shoveled the food into my mouth. I was anxious to see Yurgi, too.

***

While we walked along the cement walkways and into the polished halls of the hospital, I told Elsa the story of Yurgi's rooster battle. She listened carefully, a slight smile on her lips.

"I'm sure we can straighten all this out," she said as she guided us into Yurgi's room. "Here's your family, Yurgi."

Relief flooded Yurgi's lonely little face, and he flew from his hospital bed to give each of us big hugs. Tears brimmed in my eyes as I squeezed my little one. I'd missed him.

"We will soon get you out of here," Elsa said to Yurgi and patted his head. Then she headed toward the door. "While you visit, I'll find Yurgi's doctor. He needs to hear your rooster story."

Papa and Taty sat on the bed with Yurgi snuggled between them. Alya and I were too excited to sit.

"Yurgi," I exclaimed and grabbed his hands, "we have shoes for you. Elsa brought them."

"And a sweater," Alya continued, "and stockings and new pants."

Yurgi's eyes sparkled in his flushed face.

"You will not look like a poor immigrant when we enter America," I said.

We chattered on about all that had happened to us. Our hearts were light, knowing Elsa would straighten things out. Even Taty joined in, but Papa just sat there, listening. I wondered why he was so quiet. I could hear Elsa in the hall with a man, but their words were in English. I shrugged. It meant nothing to me.

Before long Elsa returned, "Visiting hours are over for the morning," she said.

Yurgi's face immediately clouded.

"I'll bring your family back real soon," she hastened to add and then smiled warmly at Yurgi. Tears were streaming down Yurgi's cheeks, but he smiled and waved good-bye.

As we walked back, Elsa's thoughts seemed far away, but she tried to make conversation. She pointed to the big buildings across the water, "That's New York City. It's in New York State. New York is one of the forty-eight states of America. And over there," Elsa said, pointing to the left, "is a state called New Jersey."

"And we are hoping to join our German-Russian friends in a state called Wisconsin," Papa said, suddenly breaking the silence that had enveloped him since our hospital visit.

"Wonderful," Elsa exclaimed as some of her sparkle returned. "That means you will have to take a ferry to New Jersey to board your train, and you will be able to go through a very special door."

"What special door?" I asked. "Is Papa's door to America a real door?"

Papa laughed and said, "Oh, Lisenka, I only meant we had to go through Ellis Island to get to America. But, Elsa, what door are you talking about?"

"It's just an ordinary door to exit to the ferry, but the words painted on it make it wonderful. They say, 'Push: To America.' Thousands of immigrants have pushed hard to get to America. That's their last 'push' to get in."

She looked at me. "Did you have to push hard to get here?"

I nodded, but said nothing. There had been too much pushing to explain in a few words now.

A frown flickered across her face. Then she smiled and said, "Let's begin your English lesson." She took a pad of paper and a pencil from her pocket. "Push: To America," she wrote. Then, pointing to each word, she sounded them out in this strange, new language: "Push: To America."

I fastened my eyes on the words and repeated them. Alya tried, too. I must remember every lesson in this new language with the strange looking words, I thought.

Back at our room, Elsa hugged Taty and Alya; she shook Papa's hand and gave him a strange look. He nodded. Then she tore the paper from the pad and handed it to me. "Here, Lisenka," she said. "You practice your English lesson until I return."

Carefully, I took the paper and sat on my bed, staring at it and whispering the words over and over.

I barely noticed Papa follow Elsa from the room, but when he returned a few minutes later, his lips were pressed into a grim smile—a look I could not miss.

"We have gone through much together, and now I must share the truth with you," Papa said. "It is as I overheard." His fists were clenched while he paced the floor. We waited, afraid, silent.

Anger filled his voice. He seemed to spit out the words: "The doctor knows Yurgi does not have ringworm. That is just an excuse, a lie to keep us from entering America. I heard the doctor say that more poor immigrants are not needed here. He said there were too many of our kind here already. He called us leeches, ready to suck the life out of America! How can one man have the power to block our way?"

Papa sat down on his bed, suddenly tired.

Leeches? I had a leech on my leg once. As I stood in the water's edge fishing, it had stuck to my leg and begun to suck my blood.

"How can we be leeches, Papa?" I asked, disgusted. "What does he mean?"

Now Papa's voice was smooth. "The doctor has seen thousands of immigrants like us pass through Ellis Island. He has seen too many; hatred now blinds him to the truth. He thinks we will rob America of her wealth, that we will not work, but cling to the government for food and clothes.

"He seeks any excuse to reject immigrants," Papa continued. "Unfortunately, he has found a reason, bad as it is, to reject us . . . and hate us."

"Elsa knows he's lying," I gasped. "She will help us push in."

"Elsa will try," Papa said sadly, "But she does not have the power to stop the doctor. He has already signed our rejection papers. And she does not have much time. Tomorrow our ship sets sail . . . back to the Old Country."

Rejection papers? Back to Russia? But America is in sight. I looked once more at the words on my precious sheet of paper. "Push: To America" became bleary. As my eyes filled with tears, the words seemed to wash away.

Chapter 25

While the day's light was fading from the room, I lay curled up on my bed, facing the wall. The hours had dragged by since Papa had shared his news. At first, my tears had seemed endless. Now my eyes were dry, burning. My throat burned, too, and my legs and arms felt heavy . . . so did my heart.

Papa, Taty, and Alya had gone to visit Yurgi, but I did not go. I wanted to be alone. I smoothed Elsa's paper. It had become wrinkled in my sweaty hand, and the words were faded, but I could still read them. Ja, I could read them—in English. Once more I whispered, "Push: To America."

I sighed. I want to push, but how can I? Suddenly, I remembered Papa's words on the ship, "We are all just weak people. Only God can give us strength."

I rolled my eyes, wondering how I could be so slow to learn God's lessons. Of course, I realized, only God can give me strength. I folded my hands and began to pray softly.

"Dear Lord, you have fought many battles for us. Sometimes, too, we are soldiers, fighting for you, but always you are the one who gives us the strength. Please, do not leave us on our own now. We need your strength. Amen."

Then I remembered what we were fighting—the hateful doctor, the rejection papers, the ship ready to carry us back to Russia—and I quickly added, "Lord, actually, I think we really need more than strength right now. We need a miracle. Amen again."

"A miracle, ja," said a voice behind me.

I rolled over. Elsa stood by my bed, holding a tray and smiling.

"That's a big request," she said.

I was too embarrassed to talk, but Elsa didn't wait for an answer. "The Lord does promise to answer prayers," she said and sat on the edge of my bed. "Jesus says, 'Ye have not, because ye ask not.' Well, Lisenka, you really know how to ask!"

She smiled again. I couldn't help smiling back. She made me feel special.

"Here, I brought you some milk and soda crackers for your bedtime snack."

Cautiously, I sat up. The darkened room whirled and then stood still. I was glad Elsa could not see my hot face and puffy eyes. The cold milk cooled my burning throat, but I could not eat.

"Thank you, Elsa," I said. "But I am not hungry."

She set the tray on the floor. I hesitated, wanting to say more, searching for words. Then I blurted out, "And thank you, too, for all you have done for us. I will . . . never forget you."

Embarrassed at my faltering words, I flung my arms around her in a sobbing hug.

She pulled me close and then quickly pushed me away. "Lisenka," she said, "You are burning up!"

"It's just from crying," I explained, more embarrassed.

Elsa was not convinced and yanked the chain on the light. She took my chin, tipping my face toward the light. Then she looked at my neck.

"Lisenka, Lisenka," she said, shaking her head.

"What is wrong?" Papa demanded, suddenly appearing in the doorway with Taty and Alya.

My heart was pounding wildly. "What is wrong with me?" I asked in a quavering voice.

Elsa turned instead to Papa, "Feel how hot she is and look at the rash on her face and neck. I'm no doctor, but I'm sure about this one. Lisenka has the measles!"

"The measles!" Papa gasped, "What does that mean?"

Taty began to cry. Alya and I joined her. How could we deal with one more thing against us?

Unexpectedly, Elsa burst into laughter. It shocked us all into silence. I stared at her, puzzled.

"I'll be right back with a doctor," she said and stepped out the door.

Taty pulled Alya down on her bed and held her tightly. Papa stood in the middle of the room mumbling, "I don't know what is going on. Lord, what is happening?"

I had seen the hope in Elsa's eyes. "Papa, be patient!" I said. "God knows what he's doing!"

***

I held my breath. The doctor stared at me, nodding his head and saying, "Ah-huh." Elsa stood at his elbow, eagerly watching every move. Finally he straightened and said a few English words to Elsa as they left the room.

"Papa," I whispered, "What did he say?"

Before Papa could answer, Elsa whirled back in. "This is wonderful!" she exclaimed. "Lisenka has the measles, a contagious disease."

"What is so wonderful about being sick?" Papa asked, impatiently. Elsa was making no sense.

She began to laugh again, unable to speak. Finally, she caught her breath. "The doctor is quarantining your whole family. You must not expose other people to the measles."

Now I understood.

"But our ship sails tomorrow?" Papa said, still searching for answers.

"Ja, it sails," Elsa said, grabbing Papa's hands. "But you will not be on it. You are not allowed to leave this room until Lisenka is well."

A deep sigh whistled through Papa's lips.

"Don't you see?" Elsa asked. "Now we have time—time to get those rejection papers reversed."

"It's a miracle," Papa said. His words were hushed.

"Ja, it is!" Elsa said, and flashed a knowing look at me.

Chapter 26

I woke up—still hot and itchy—and looked at my arms peppered with little red spots. It is not supposed to be this way, I thought. In the Bible Jesus' miracles immediately healed the sick. So why did God send me a miracle that made me sick? Maybe this isn't a miracle, but just one more problem before we are sent back to Russia. I slammed my fist into my pillow and turned over with a loud sigh.

Papa, Taty, and Alya looked up surprised. Papa had been quietly reading the Bible to them near the window. Elsa had brought a German Bible to us a couple days ago. It had been Papa's turn to have shaky hands as he reached for it; since then he had spent many hours reading in it. Taty was sitting close to him now with Alya nestled between them.

"How are you feeling now, little lady?" Papa asked cheerfully when he saw my open eyes.

I snorted and flipped back over to face the wall. I was in no mood to answer his cheerful questions.

My bed sagged. I knew Papa had planted himself behind me. I braced myself for another attack of cheerfulness. It didn't come.

Instead Papa said, "I am sorry you have been sick. At first your measles gave me hope. I thought those little red spots would bring us freedom, but it's been five days, and still Elsa cannot get a second doctor to check Yurgi. Soon our time will be gone."

The disappointment in his voice added to my own hopelessness. My throat tightened till it hurt. Elsa hadn't even visited yesterday or today; maybe she had given up, too.

Papa continued, "Perhaps God does not have in mind to give us freedom in America. He has already given us freedom from our sins through the blood of his son. That is enough freedom for us. His ways are not our ways. His thoughts are not ours. We can only trust that he's working for our good."

I didn't want to hear Papa's sermon. I remained silent, unmoved. Papa patted my stiffened back. My bed squeaked. I heard him slowly walk away, then talk softly with Taty by the window.

In the hall outside a familiar voice cut through the babble of different languages. Elsa breezed in saying, "We're close. Dr. Mikkel, the one who examined Lisenka, has finally agreed to check Yurgi."

I flipped back to see Elsa. Papa swung around, clapping his hands together. "Oh, thank you, Elsa," he said, and he rushed over to shake her hand.

"Believe me," Elsa said, raising her eyebrows, "Talking him into this wasn't easy. No doctor wants to go against what another doctor has decided, especially on this island."

"Will this doctor . . . after he sees Yurgi . . . be willing to go against another?" Papa asked, hesitantly.

"He must," Elsa answered, grinning. "He's what we need to complete our miracle. Sorry—I have to rush off. There's a group of Italians waiting for me to settle them into their rooms."

She started to run out, then stopped, remembering something. She pulled a red paper heart from her pocket and handed it to me. It had three words on it.

"You're feeling better, aren't you, Lisenka?" she asked. Then without waiting for an answer she said, "Here's your next English lesson." Elsa pointed to each word and said, first in German, then in English, "I love you." She gave me a squeeze and dashed off.

Suddenly I did feel better. I looked at the bright heart and was filled with warmth. "Papa," I said, "I'm sorry for behaving so badly. Will you forgive me?"

"Ja, little one," Papa said, tenderly. He came to me and knelt by my bed, then motioned for Taty and Alya to join him.

"We must also seek forgiveness from our heavenly Father," Papa said. "I am afraid we all behaved badly."

With closed eyes, he bowed his head. Quickly we did the same.

"Heavenly Father, you have shown us your unfailing love again and again as we journeyed to America. Thank you for always remaining with us. Please forgive us for doubting your plan to bring us safely in. I am sure it is your will that we live in America. It is here that we will have the freedom to study your Word and worship you openly. Here Lisenka and the little ones will be educated and fed; here Taty will again regain her strength! Please continue to lead us. We will follow."

Papa paused. Nobody moved. Then he continued,

"Thank you for giving us freedom from our sins. It is a freedom no man can take from us. You have given us the sure hope that heaven will some day be our home! Amen."

"Amen," I whispered and opened my eyes. The red heart fluttered in my hands. Stumbling through my three new English words, I looked at Papa and said, "I love you!"

Papa gathered us all in his arms and repeated, "I love you!"

Alya broke away from the hug, skipped around the room, and then plopped herself on top of me. With her little hands she brushed the tears from my cheeks and said, "Ahh luf ya!"

I pulled my little one close. I knew she loved me. And I knew Papa, Taty, and Yurgi loved me, but, most importantly, I knew God loved me.

Chapter 27

"Do you see them yet?" I asked Taty who was standing at the window with her hands clasped tensely behind her. She leaned forward, straining to see.

"Not yet," she said with a sigh and joined Alya and me sitting on the bench against the wall. Papa had told us to wait here in the main hall with our bundles.

"How long can it take Papa and Elsa to get Yurgi and bring him here?" I demanded and jumped up to look out the window myself.

I glanced out impatiently, then looked again. "Here they come!" I yelled and dashed toward the door. Then I remembered Papa's stern words and hurried back to the bench. He didn't want any of us to make a stir. "We will leave quietly," he had said.

When they walked in through the door, little Yurgi was in Papa's arms, but as soon as he saw us, he squirmed free and raced over. First Yurgi jumped into Taty's arms, then mine, then Alya's. Then he started over again, this time including Elsa and Papa who'd reached the bench.

We laughed, we cried, we hugged each other. It was wonderful to be all together again.

After a few minutes, Elsa said, "It is time."

Suddenly we were silent. My heart thumped against my chest. Papa handed out our bundles, then grabbed his own and his violin.

We followed Elsa. She led us through a large, crowded room and down a busy hall. Papa, carrying Yurgi, followed first. Taty and Alya were last. I walked in the middle.

The noise around us could not disturb our solemn procession. Nobody broke our silence until Elsa stopped and said, "This is it."

She looked at Papa with a twinkle in her eyes. He chuckled and stepped aside. Both their eyes were on me. I was puzzled and looked from Papa to Elsa. Elsa pointed to a door. "Lisenka, she said, "Will you please help me?"

I began to quiver with excitement. "Ja," I said, smiling at Elsa, then Papa, Taty, and the little ones. I thought, all things do work together for good! Thank you, God!

I took a deep breath, raised my hand, and stepped forward. The three words painted on the door seemed to welcome us. "Push: To America," I said in English and then led the way through the door.